THE DROVER'S CURSE

BY BOB HARVEY

Copyright 2022

Paperback ISBN: 978-1-953686-14-5
eBook ISBN: 978-1-953686-15-2

Library of Congress Control Number: 2022940967

Living Springs
Publishers

WWW.LivingSpringsPublishers.com
Centennial, CO

Dedication

Dedicated to those who lived, or wished they could have lived, the life of a frontier cowboy.

Ahh, to be able to live up to J.R.R. Tolkien's "Not all who wander are lost".

Acknowledgements

Nothing can adequately express my gratitude to my wife, Judy, for listening....endlessly.

Special thanks to Wichita, Kansas for hosting the Cowtown's anniversary celebrations of the Chisholm Trail. The events put the meat on the bones of the often overly-romanticized life of the drover.

THE DROVER'S CURSE...

It was one of those rare occasions where my father returned home early enough for the two of us to sit on the porch and talk. The topics were almost always about the goings-on at the fort, being a cavalry soldier and the challenges of being an officer. Each sentence was generally followed by extended moments of silence while the words settled in and new thoughts were developing. Most times I was surprised by the content and intensity.

"Dark, beady, close-set, little eyes," the Lieutenant whispered. His words were barely audible, even with an evening that seemed quieter than usual.

"What about 'em?" I asked when it became clear he had finished the sentence.

"There are a couple of those men that I am going to have to watch very closely."

He leaned back in his favorite old, creaking rocking chair, staring off across the Parade Grounds at the two companies of new recruits that arrived that day at Fort Scott.

We were sitting on the front porch of

Officers Quarters #1 which was home to our family...him, Mother and me.

From my favorite perch on the first step off the porch I was trying desperately to keep the conversation going. These typically brief man-on-man conversations were hard to come by...and most were <u>very</u> short-lived.

"Why?"

"They have dark, beady eyes. Seems that every time I have a significant issue at the fort, it involves somebody with dark, beady, little eyes. I find myself being wary of those with that trait and being wary has served me well over the years. I suggest you use great care when you deal with those with dark, beady eyes as you go through life. Enough said," his voice trailed off leaving no room for further discussion.

***

"I'm in this mess because of these goddamn boots! Things started going to hell the day I put them on!"

Strange the things you think of when you're in deep, serious trouble. I find myself totally at the mercy of an adversary with dark, beady, little eyes that were staring directly into mine.

His eyes moved ever so slightly to the right, still not blinking. Even in the bright sunlight he wasn't squinting. He just kept glaring at me. There was no doubt he was trying to figure out what to do next. Every couple of seconds he would straighten up a bit and move slowly toward me but then he would stop and retreat. I had no doubt that he knew I was helpless.

I'm lying head down, on my back, about halfway down a steep dirt bank that bottoms out far below. This had to be one of the deepest ravines in the Arickaree Breaks. He's still just crouched there ......the biggest, longest, angriest rattlesnake I had ever seen and he was just a couple of feet from my left ear. My right ear was full of cactus needles. All I can see is up...right into the blazing sun, except for what was being partially blocked by the toes of those damned two-week-old show-off boots. Framing the sun like they are, they looked like the horns of the devil himself.

Not too long ago I was walking northwest through what I figured was the sand hills of Kansas Territory, but I could have been in Colorado or even Nebraska, who can tell out there, when I heard hoof beats coming up fast somewhere in the hills behind me.

This particular hillside was about the only place in this part of the territory that didn't have much cover to hide in. I decided the smart thing to do was to jump off the edge of the gully, make my way to the bottom and find some place to hunker down until these guys went away. I didn't know who they were, but I knew they had been following me for at least two days. Back of my mind I figured it was probably two or three of the guys who recovered one of my borrowed horses in Abilene. That's Kansas, not Texas. If it was them, I hoped they hadn't found where I hid my saddlebags, scabbard and Sharps rifle.

The riders were close enough that I could hear the horses snorting so I figured I was clean out of time. I jumped the edge of the cut and into the gully. Then I set my heels to slow down.

Now, if I would have been wearing my old boots, or even new boots that had a working heel, I would have dug them in, checked my fall and been able to work through the sagebrush and rocks to get to the bottom.

But when I bought these new boots in St. Joes, I was more concerned about looking dandy rather than sliding down a gully. The riding heel on these damned boots just turned into a pair of barrel staves on these hardscrabble hillsides. Down the slope I went, ass-over-elbows right up until the moment my foot got caught in sagebrush and I jerked to a stop...... upside down and backward.

I could tell my right foot was caught up in sagebrush as I had no movement in that leg...it was stretched out straight. Sagebrush and gravity had me pinned to the hillside. My left leg was free but close to that rattler. Every little movement caused him to get more agitated and noisier. He was every bit of six foot in length...and a foot and a half of him was stretched into the coil, ready to strike. The only motion he made was flicking that forked pink tongue with the black tips.

There was no doubt those riders would track me to the edge of the break. Then they would spy my boot prints going down the grade. What they wouldn't expect to see is me strung up like a beef carcass waitin' for the butcher.

I had a pretty good hold on a palm-sized sandstone rock with my right hand and I was trying to convince myself that I could flip it over in the general direction of the rattler. I was almost certain that doing so would catch his attention for a second or two and maybe I could pull myself loose.

Since I'm on such a steep angle, I'm

hoping I can kick my leg up over my head and I'll somersault again, head-over-heels down the hill just like I came in. That's assuming that my right leg will pull loose of the sagebrush and come along for the ride. If it doesn't, the only target those fangs will have is my butt or my crotch.

I was glad I had taken the time to put on my chaps. If any part of me was to become a target to that rattler, I would hope it would be that part wrapped in leather.

"That low-life coward is drawing a bead on a defenseless man."

I had just about got my courage up when I realized a shadow had settled on my face. There, right between the toes of my damned new boots, is the silhouette of a man. He's just standing on the edge of the ravine, staring down at me.

I would have gone for my Colt but I could tell from the way the holster was laying that it was empty. The revolver was probably half-full of dirt anyway, wherever it was. Looking up at him through the toes of my boots I couldn't help but notice they looked just like the rear sights on my Sharps, which, of course, I didn't have either.

From the shadow came a strange high-pitched cackle that sounded like something between laughter and pain. I watched as he took his rifle to his shoulder.

Now in recent years I have been a target enough times to develop an appropriate sense of urgency while under fire. Urgency was surely appropriate at this time. *"NOW"*.

With every ounce of strength I could muster I jerked my knees up and threw my left leg over my head. My right leg pulled loose from the sagebrush but before I finished my first complete turn, I heard the report from his rifle. The echo down through the break made a sound much like those cannons they shot at us in the war down south. I was waiting to feel the slug go into whatever part of my body was up at the time it got there.

My back. Right between the shoulder blades. The impact forced every bit of air out of my lungs and then replaced it with agony. Worst pain I ever felt. I was afraid I was gut-shot and would lie there bleeding for a long time before I died. Instead, from what I was feeling, the lead must have gone right through my lungs.

My mind began to clear and I realized I was on my back on a slab rock in the bottom of the wash. I inherently reached around to find the wound but instead found a small round rock that had taken my full weight, jamming between my backbone and my right shoulder blade. I lay there still trying to breath, eyes closed tightly and wondering about the severity of the wound.

Sound and motion. I made myself open my eyes. The now headless rattler was writhing and thrashing as it tumbled down the hillside. It fell into sagebrush about a foot away.

"Shot its damned head clean off, he did. From way up there he hit a moving target about the size of a silver dollar. He was making a point, I'm thinking.... or maybe just showing off...but WHO is he? No. That's not the question. WHERE is he? Squinting into the sunshine again, nothing. No sign of anyone up on the ridge. How can that be?"

THE BOOTS

Two nights in St. Joseph, Missouri. That's just about all I can afford when I come off a drive. Where I go, the whiskey costs almost as much as the women, so that last bit of silver I get for my final pay goes away quickly.

I checked the jingle in my pocket and started down toward the railroad loading chutes. The men down there always seem to know what outfit is coming in.

At this point in a drive, many of the hands will have had enough of the trail and will take their last pay and head home... or anywhere else, just as long as it doesn't smell or look like a steer.

While walking down 4th I noticed that one more piece of the leather on my boots was about to give way. Probably every one of my toes has seen the light of day sometime in the last couple of months. The soles of both boots were barely more than the thickness of a sheet of newspaper.

As if by providence I found myself in front of "Richard Moore and Sons. Purveyors of High-Quality Custom Boots and other leather goods". I knew better that to look in the window but there I was, shading my eyes so I could gaze at the inventory.

Right smack dab in front of me was the finest, shiniest pair of boots that I ever laid eyes on.

The little, smart part of my brain said if I buy them, I'd have to eat them because I won't have a dime for a meal.

The bigger, slower part says, "damn, would I look jaunty in those boots".

Now over the years I have been told by some of my occasional female acquaintances that I have some qualities that border on handsome. Recently though, I haven't garnered much attention from the fairer sex. I came to the conclusion that it is probably because of my old worn-out boots. I guess, though, if I were to be honest, it might be that I usually need a haircut, shave, bath, a laundry...and some money.

There is an age-old belief that every stitch in a boot weakens the leather so a man should stay away from fancy stitches and go with good leather. As I'm staring at the boots in the window, I'm thinking that stitching makes those boots look about as fancy as anything I've ever owned.

At that very moment, out from the door,

steps one Mr. Moore. "Come on in here drover, we have lots for you to see."

Now, let's agree on something here. There isn't a leather shop in the world that doesn't smell good. That smell draws men...even calls their name. Almost makes you feel like you are already three drinks into a once-full whiskey bottle... euphoria... yep, that's it. Feelin' good.

"Figure you're about an eleven-and-a-half. That right?" said Mr. Moore, looking down at my bedraggled boots.

"Naw." I replied. "I'm really a ten-and-a-half...I just got a good deal on these a year or so back, so I stuffed 'em to make 'em work."

Most of that is the truth...the part that ain't is that I found those boots, sittin' on a riverbank somewhere around Ada, Oklahoma. Since they weren't being worn or even tended to at the moment, I figured they was left behind and I decided to give them a new life. That was during one of those times that I was on horseback and I could move on with some haste. For some reason, unfortunately, I have a tendency to be without a horse many times.

"Well, I'm sure you know that isn't good for your feet," Mr. Moore responded sternly, "and for someone of your age, you have a lot of life ahead of you and you need your feet and knees. What are you, about 24?"

"Nope, I'm 31."

"Sure don't look it."

"Thanks. Uh, how much are those boots in the window?"

"Those are our best. They are eleven dollars in most colors and thirteen in others."

As I unconsciously jingled my remaining cash, Mr. Moore sensed the situation.

"You know, I have a grand pair of boots very similar to these that were ordered by a gentleman that only wore them for about two hours."

"Why was that?"

"Combination of a bad hand, fast whiskey and a slow draw."

"They be my size?"

"Yes, I believe they are."

He disappeared into the store and came back out with the boots. Dark chestnut in color, some stitching but not too much. Perfect, except for the #5 riding heel.

I'm thinking to myself, *I have always preferred a working heel as it holds a spur and sits solid in the stirrup. If you're just out for a leisurely ride that riding heel looks good but if you're herding cattle 14 hours a day, it ain't for the job. More important is that you don't have much heel under you when walking on uneven ground.*

"Seems as if you might be a bit concerned about the heel. I know it takes some getting used to, but spur shanks set good on them and their cut is easy on the horse and fender. Right stylish too, aren't they?"

"Never been too awful concerned about style. Just don't like to fall down."

Mr. Moore offered me a pair of new cotton stockings to wear while trying on the boots...they slipped on almost without me touching them. They felt so good and natural that I smiled and took a couple springy steps that could have been viewed as a "yes, I have to have them" signal.

I heard myself whisper, "How much?" sending yet another signal that says, "I don't have much to work with."

"Well, I like you," replied Mr. Moore, looking me straight in the eye. "What can you pay?"

"I've still got to buy a horse so I can get back on with some outfit going north," I explained, "I could probably go six dollars," fully expecting him to come back at eight.

"Just leave them on and keep the stockings," he replied.

I was just about to protest his generosity when another shopkeeper came in and asked how much Mr. Moore would pay for the pair of walking shoes that he was carrying. Mr. Moore said he would look at them and get back to him later in the day.

That very distinguished gentleman was just barely out the door when Mr. Moore called to a young man that had stepped behind the sales counter, "Jeremiah, clean these walking shoes up, polish them and then take three dollars over to Mr. Holt," he directed.

I was in the final stages of making up my mind when Mr. Moore again called to the young man, "And, Son, please discard this gentleman's boots, he will no longer be needing them...and also, please discard his, uh, stockings."

Now I clearly had no choice but to buy the boots.

A few minutes later, out on the boardwalk I went, striding and grinning.

I stopped at the edge of the walk, waiting for a wagon and team to pass before stepping down into the street. I looked up to see where the sun was in the sky and the sign on the store next to Moore's caught my attention, "Holt's Undertaking and Funerals". Now, I ain't the fastest Horned Toad in the creek bed but it didn't take long to figure out why I got such a great deal.

NELSON STORY AND HIS MONTANA DRIVE

It took quite a while to get to the railroad yards. Before I would have just slogged down the street, not worrying what I was stepping in. Now, with my new property, I had to be careful.

Once I got down there, one of the hands with the Atchison, Topeka and Santa Fe told me to talk with a couple of cowhands that were sitting on the edge of the loading dock. As I walked carefully toward them, I recognized one of them as Sam Kitzel, a drover I worked with on one of the Santa Fe Trail herds a year or so back.

"Hey, Sam."

"Well, I never," snorted old Sam.

"I'm sure you did," was a good reply for that greeting and I used it without even thinking.

"Who told you that?" Sam replied, lowering his gaze.

"Nobody in particular," I said, sensing there was additional, and probably bad, news coming.

"You need to know; I didn't do it."

"But you know who did and you didn't tell me."

"Yep. That's right. I should have let you know."

"So? Who was it?" I asked, waiting for more information so I could figure out who and what I was supposed to be mad about.

"Carleton."

"Figures! You know where he is now?"

"Actually, he came in off the Goodnight-Loving last night, picked up his pay and headed uptown to Madeline's."

"He's still got that dim-wit brother riding next to him and now a third disciple.... a skinny-as-a-rail fellow that carries a big Bowie......don't like the looks of him. Nervous. Always looking around like he expects to see somebody he don't like. Little beady eyes. Won't look you in the eye. Evil. Yup. That's what he is. Evil."

"I'll go find Carleton. Sam, can you get me on a drive up north with anybody?"

"Texas cattleman by the name of Nelson Story has a big herd heading north to Montana. His trail boss just bought some yearlings from Armour and he is going to add them to a herd that he's puttin' together somewhere in Nebraska. If you want I'll give you my mark and I'm sure he'll put you on."

"I'd appreciate the mark. Now, let me go

find Carleton," all the time wondering why I was supposed to find him.

"Don't shoot him. Law here in Missouri is really tight and even a horse thief can't be shot."

"Uh-huh." Now it was starting to make sense. "So, you know what he rode in on?"

"Big, slow Paint."

"Do you know where it is?"

"Over at Sunderland's Livery, I reckon."

"Has he still got my Sharps Repeater and my scabbard?"

"I reckon."

"Well, Sam, here's how you're going to make peace with me."

"What do you have in mind?"

"When you see Carleton tell him I came to collect my property and replace the horse that he stole from me in Dodge. Tell him that he better not come after me because once I'm away from the law here in Missouri, I won't be the least bit concerned about killing a horse thief."

"I will do that just so I can have some peace of mind."

"I'm okay with you now, Sam, but I also want you to tell him, if he asks, that I'm headed back to Texas."

"OK by me."

"Thanks for the information and the

mark. Both are appreciated."

Less than an hour later I was back in the saddle, with my Beecher Bible Rifle in the scabbard, on a good horse that was now mine, and I was headed for Nebraska to sign on with a drive. Oh, and my boots were sitting pretty in the stirrups...those glorious boots.

THE RIDE TOWARD NEBRASKA

Crossing Kansas, even with wandering Indians and a pretty good sampling of petty criminals, is a pretty easy trip. There are enough towns and settlements to provide some hospitality and the trails are damn near flat.

I rode alongside of the Atchison, Topeka and Santa Fe tracks for most of the way, took a turn to the south and west to Abilene...that's Kansas, not Texas...and then from there I reckoned I would turn northwest, headed for the Arickaree Breaks...the point where the Colorado, Kansas and Nebraska territories meet. Railroads are starting to tie into other routes and pretty soon it will be easy to get to most places west of the Mississippi and east of the Rockies.

Abilene is a real cow town. Railroads, livestock, cattlemen, drovers, gamblers, lonely women and shysters of all types all combined to create general confusion, a lot of noise and more than a few opportunities to get into trouble.

I concluded the only thing that was

keeping me from having the world by the tail was cash. My three dollars would go away fast in Abilene so I needed a card game. The big games in the sporting houses weren't what I wanted as they were watched way too closely, and my skills weren't up to the standards necessary to insure my success. I found a saloon a block from the main line. Four tables in the back with an opening at each.

When I walked into the room, everybody looked up from their cards. There seemed to be an uneasy quiet and I soon figured I needed to ask what was going on.

"A fellow was just in here with two other men and they were looking for a horse thief," explained one of the players, "said they was going to keep walking and talking until they found him and then they would kill the scoundrel and anybody that was with him."

"What's the name of the guy he is looking for, did he say?"

"Clyde Driscoll."

"Any of you know Clyde? Probably ought to let him know."

"Never heard of him. Nobody else has either."

"Well, not much a man can do then, is there? Let's play poker."

With that the games began again but everybody kept their eye on the door... and the stranger with the new boots.

Three hours, two rye whiskeys and fourteen dollars in new assets later, Clyde pushed himself back from the table, thanked the remaining players for their hospitality, excused himself and walked into the streets of Abilene.

"Not a bad night's work," I whispered to myself.

Since I had recent history with the process of recovering a horse from a stable, I thought I should check on my own property at Hahn's Livery. It was dark and I was concerned about keeping my boots out of the unpleasant material in the streets. If it hadn't been for that concern, I probably would have seen that Hahn's wagon and horse were still hitched to the rail outside of the stable...and I wouldn't have walked in without knowing what was going on.

VISITING WITH AUGUST CARLETON, HIS BROTHER AND A CLOSE FRIEND

Not much light comes off a kerosene lantern with an old wick and a smoky chimney. I could see some blankets thrown on the floor as I walked deeper into the barn. Then I realized those weren't blankets. Old Man Hahn was laying there in the darkness.

I called his name and bent over to check on him. Next thing I knew I was working on becoming conscious, arms tied on the stall boards, half standing up, half falling down. Right there in front of me was a skinny guy that looked and acted much like a weasel. Head bobbing around, peering around the stable while, at the same time, keeping a close watch on me.

"Hey Boss, he's coming 'round."

Out of the shadow appeared August Carleton, a little rounder than the last time I saw him but with that same ol' menacing grin across his face.

"Well, well, Clyde. Good of you to join us. Isn't it, boys?"

Nobody called Carlton by his first name because he is said to have killed at least a couple of fellows for playing with his name of August. He was simply Carleton to those who knew him. Don't know that he had any friends, at least never heard anybody speak highly of him.

"Clyde, do you have any idea on how my horse came to be here in Abilene when it was supposed to be in St. Joes?"

"Carleton, you know for a fact that you stole my horse in Dodge City. Several people saw you ride out of town on it. I was just recovering some assets to offset my loss."

"You can pretty it up with whatever words you want to, but it still comes down to you being a horse-thief."

"Don't know that there is much I can do if you want to take back your horse. Just leave my saddle bags, rifle and scabbard when you go."

"Oh, I've already got the horse. That's why Hahn is resting on the floor. He, for some reason, thought that my horse was yours and he took exception to me walking it out the door."

"Hope you didn't hurt him too much. He's a nice man and he's gotta be in his 60's."

"Don't care. Don't think he's dead. Braden didn't hit him that hard. Now, there is the issue of my saddlebags, rifle and scabbard. Don't seem to be around. You going to tell me?"

"They were here in the corner of the stall when I left a couple of hours ago. Either you got them or some other thief already stole them."

"Them are some damn-fool, stupid words from somebody hanging around like you are."

I had been watching a lone rider coming down the street, visible to me over Carleton's shoulder. He dismounted and quietly walked his horse to a point just outside of the stable door.

"Look, Carleton, if I give you my gear...including my Sharps, will you let me go? I'm done with the herds. I'm going to Colorado to try my luck in the gold fields. You'll never see me again."

He studied my face for a bit, "I expect that if I kill you I won't ever know where your gear is."

He told his brother Braden to untie me and as soon as I had both hands free, I went to check on Hahn. He was bloodied up pretty bad but was just coming around when the rider I saw on the street walked in. Even in the dim light, I could see his shiny Texas Ranger badge. I began to feel much better.

The Ranger went over and lit another lamp. After surveying the scene, he came over to Hahn.

"Old timer, who did this to you?"

Hahn used an unsteady hand to wave toward Carleton, Braden and the Weasel.

"What are you doing here?" the Ranger asked, staring straight into my eyes.

I was quick to explain that I heard the ruckus and came over to check on Hahn. He asked if I had a horse in the stable and I told him that was my carriage and horse outside, all the while looking Hahn straight in the eye so he knew I would mean no harm when I borrowed it to get to the outskirts of town.

"You need to go on about your business then. I'm going to do a little more work here and then I'll take care of your friend," ordered the Ranger.

I walked out, got up on Hahn's carriage and skedaddled as fast as I could without appearing to be running away. My friends back there knew better than to raise any additional suspicions by challenging my departure. I'm sure they were also thinking they would go over to the hotel and recover my personal property as soon as they talked their way out of the situation. I pulled up to a hitching post at the last watering hole in Abilene. I walked in, tossed down a Rye, walked out, picked out a horse and hit the trail.

"Nobody in there is going to be able to ride in the condition they're in. Most of them won't remember if they were on their horse when they came in anyway," I excused my actions as I hit the crossroads, looked up a clear moonlit sky.... *"Let's see, moon is there, so that way is north, adios Abilene".*

BACK ON THE TRAIL

I probably should have taken the time to lift the hooves on the horses. If I had I probably wouldn't have picked the sorrel I "borrowed". One shoe was already gone and one was so loose that it wasn't going to hold on for long.

I turned the horse loose and, as I suspected, he turned to return to town. *In a couple of hours it will be daybreak and he'll wander into Abilene. Somebody will recognize him and get him to his rightful owner.*

I figured I was about ten miles away from both Abilene and trouble. I got off the trail, found a big Rabbit bush and made myself go down for sleep. I was going to be on foot in the brush so needed to rest.

Daylight, birds chirping, and a neighing horse all combined to wake me. I set up just enough to look around and try to figure out why a horse was out here, hopefully without a rider.

No such luck. There was a rider on the horse and they were about a half-mile or so back. Since he had his head down, looking at the ground, he appeared to be tracking something....and it occurred to me that the something might be me.

I stayed motionless behind the bush. Eventually the rider stood up in the stirrups, surveyed the area, sat back in the saddle and reined his horse almost straight west. I was pretty certain that in a couple of minutes he would be out of my view and then I'd disappear deeper into the brush.

The only property I owned at that moment was hanging on my hips. My Colt 45 was in the holster on my right hip and my chaps were flapping in the breeze that is forever blowing across the prairie. I couldn't help but smile when I thought how well things worked out back at Hahn's. I got away with only a sore shoulder and a bruise on my left wrist.

***

Back in Abilene, Carleton and his henchmen will never look under the hay in the loft for my bags, scabbard and rifle. Even if they thought about looking there, I had burrowed under that hay all the way to the very end of the loft, cached the gear and burrowed back out, tossing the hay so it looked untouched. Right smart of me, it was. Once I get back off the Story drive I'll come back to Abilene, climb back into Hahn's hay and get my gear before I head to wherever I'll be going.

JUST BEFORE THE FALL

Four straight days of walking in the heat and new boots made me ready to get a bath and get out of the cowhide. My chaps were rubbing me raw and with every step my boots were reminding me they were new. Even with a day's ride from a freighter, I was tired of walking.

Interesting how a person that makes their livelihood on horseback finds himself walking as much as I do.

Timing was good since I found myself looking down on a little settlement they call Saint Francis. I don't get the religious connection because this surely ain't no heaven. It does set on the edge of a pretty nice stretch of the Republican but otherwise I can't see much of a reason to be here if you aren't in cattle, one way or another.

When you're on foot out here, it's a good idea to sneak into town and then slip onto the streets so it appears you really do have a horse that you have tied up somewhere. Being on foot and new in town is a bad combination. Slapping the dust off my outfit, I tucked in my shirt. Then I took off my bandana and polished up my new boots so they looked all shiny. I skulked through an alley and when I was sure there wasn't anybody watching I stood up straight and strolled into the street.

Saint Francis is on the southernmost edge of the Arickaree Breaks. Somewhere in this giant rolling, rutted landscape is that place where Colorado, Nebraska and Kansas all meet. I hear that somewhere out there a government surveyor set a post with a marker on it but nothing in the surrounding area tells a man where that post is.

There are several tracks of cattle drives that have been through the breaks...best to walk on them as they are mostly level. Experienced drovers don't want their cattle going up and down into the gullies and washes as it wears them out, they lose weight, and it is easy to lose stock. They also know all the shallows at the rivers and creeks where you can take a herd without drowning half of them. All good things to know when you're on foot......especially in new boots with a too-small heel. Well-used cattle trails make it easy to walk. For that reason alone, it was foolish of me getting away from this trail and heading back into the sage.

Since I left Saint Francis, I was keeping

my eye on some dust back a mile or two. Not enough dust for it to be cattle but too much for a dust-devil kickup. Every time I hit a high spot I could see the track but every time it seemed to be about the same distance away. Twice I could see a rider and, on one occasion, it was obvious there was another rider farther back but seeming to follow the same route...right toward me. Given the situation, I wasn't in the mood for company.

I know from experience that since I wasn't following a trail I could make much better time, even on foot, than somebody tracking me on horseback. Tracking in brush takes time.

I took my bandana off, as the color red, in any amount, stands out in the brush. I also started carrying my old Stetson because it took up more top space than two of my heads. In most cases, it's also not a good idea to go down into a wash because when you climb back out the other side you leave tracks that even a blind man can see.

Running out of water when you are out here in the hills is bad for any number of reasons, not the least of which is thirst. I clambered up one of the higher hills so I could try to spot some green trees anywhere. Out here, where there are green trees, there is water. About two miles away, in what I reckoned was a mostly northerly direction, was a big stand of what looked like Cottonwood trees. That stand immediately became my destination. I turned and looked back south, hoping not to see whoever was following me into Nebraska. Now it appeared that the two riders had met up. Hard to know what to make of it, if anything.

"They might not even know I'm out here," I said to myself. *"Maybe they're just going up to get a job on the Story drive, just like me."*

While I was standing there and talking to myself like a damned fool, I heard the echoing report of a carbine. The two riders were now one...and he lit out in a westerly direction as fast as a man can ride in that country.

Off to the east a lone rider rode into view. He warily approached the horse with the empty saddle and after sitting for a few moments, he dismounted, and I couldn't see him any longer.

"Nope, not drovers," I whispered to the wind.

Another shot echoed across the landscape.

"Definitely not drovers."

The dust trailing across the prairie southwest of my perch was a sure sign that the rider who got away was still going hard.

THE POND STOP

With everything that just happened, it was important to get over to the Cottonwoods. The plan was to get some water in me and then get as far away as soon as I can.

It appeared from the top of the hill, that there was one break that would take me almost all the way to the trees. I chose to get down to the bottom and use the twisted, deep channels to provide some cover. If whoever shot the rider back there was aware of my presence, he would eventually top out on this same hill and look around. If I were on the edge of the breaks I would stand out like a peacock in a chicken yard.

It was getting close to sunset when I got to the end of the wash. I clambered five feet up a clay bank and there I found seven or eight Cottonwoods surrounding one of the prettiest little ponds I had seen in quite some time. I took a quick look around the banks and didn't find anything but game tracks, no horses. Good news if you're hiding. Two long drinks of cool, relatively clear water cleaned out half an acre of trail dust from my mouth and throat. I walked completely around each of the trees looking for marks or any other evidence that this was a popular place for riders. Nothing. No fire rings, no carving, no shredded bark, no nothing.

One of the trees had some old branches that had died off and I decided to use them to climb the tree. The dense, big leaves of the Cottonwood afforded me some hiding spaces and soon, about 14 or 15 feet above the ground, I had an open look at the surrounding hills... Nothing! Not a whiff of dust or any movement indicating somebody was out there...but I knew there was.

Now, down out of the tree. Take off those boots that don't look shiny anymore. Wrestle out of the chaps and gun belt. Dive into the pond fully dressed. That way you can bath and do your laundry at the same time, in case you have to hurry. I finally talked myself into believing that I could take my time. With nobody close I could take off the clothing and rub it between my hands to get the trail dirt loosened and rinsed out.

The ever-present breeze was growing into a northerly wind. Since it had been uncomfortably hot for days, it was almost chilly squatting in the pool, water up to my chin and I was enjoying the comfort afforded by water. I was just about to stand up and make my way out of the pool when a good-sized snake of about five foot came down to the edge of the water and slipped into the pond for a swim. He just kept coming directly toward me and once I knew for sure he was a Bull Snake and not a rattler I considered him to be a friend and I gave him a name. Dinner.

Right hand up through the water, fingers around the tail, get him in the air, quick snap like a whip and a main course was ready to skin and cook.

The wind was both a blessing and a curse. Hard to get what little kindling was available to burn but once I had a visible flame, the wind was spreading the smoke from the fire in such a swirling manner that it would have been impossible for anybody to see the smoke at this time of night....small fire so not much light, cooked my visitor and climbed the tree, used my chaps to create a nest and it's off to sleep.

DAYBREAK

Hoof beats! That will get the attention of a man, even if he is sound asleep. The morning quiet and coolness allowed me to hear them coming hard in my direction. I grabbed my chaps out of the crotch of the tree, hurried down to about six feet above the ground and jumped. Carrying the chaps would slow me down while I walked so I took the time to put them on.

I headed north, darting between the largest bushes. Be fast but stealthy.

I covered about two miles and was rounding a small hillock densely covered with undergrowth, so I slithered through to get a look at what was behind me.

Dust. Can't get an eyeball on the riders but enough dust for two. One is a mile or so back of the first. Both moving fast.

By now I had to be in Nebraska, maybe Colorado. That seemed important to me for some reason.

A cook on one of my drives said, "it's important to know you are lost when you don't know where you are." I sat there, chin deep in weeds and staring into the brush, once again trying to make sense of what he had said but, at the same time, thinking how true it was. I felt like my best chance to get away was to get to the Breaks about a half mile away. I headed there as fast as my new boots would run.

SAVED AGAIN

While I was lying at the bottom of that giant damned gully, trying desperately to get some air into my lungs I had a premonition that things were coming to an end one way or the other. In taking stock of the situation, I came to the conclusion that I had some sharpshooter that was very near and who he is, I didn't know. I had at least one other rider that had been tracking me for days and why he was, I didn't know. What I did know was that the Rattler that was my biggest concern a few minutes ago was lying beside me, headless and body twitching as life escaped him. I rolled onto my side to see how much blood I had lost.

What? No blood? Nothing? I'm not bleeding? I'm not shot?

My moment of relief was cut short when I heard the unmistakable sound of a rifle being cocked and a bullet being moved into the chamber. I knew right then I shouldn't have brought up the subject.

I heard my lips whisper "Who's there"?
Silence.

I set up, looked up and down the ditch

and then, warily, stood up.

Louder. "Who's there?"

From behind a small wash about 20 yards away, the rifleman stepped out into the open. The weasel...with beady, little, dark eyes.

Kitzel was right. This man is evil.

"Glad to see somebody I know," I said, hoping a conversation might keep him from shooting me just for the hell of it.

"No. I don't think you are."

"Carleton with you?"

"Carleton's dead. Wasn't smart enough to avoid a showdown."

"With who?"

"Doesn't matter."

"Got an extra horse that I can buy from you?"

"You ain't going no place."

"Why have you been following me?"

"Carleton and I been trackin' you. He wanted his property. I want to end you."

"I told you both that the property was at the stable the last time I saw it."

"When Carleton was bleeding out, he said to take his gear, now it's mine....and he said if I can find you and get the stuff you took, it was mine too. Then just before he died he said to take the money that was in his saddlebags as pay for killing you."

"I'll give you everything I have if you will let me live. Nobody will ever know."

"Don't care if nobody knows. From the looks of you, you don't have anything I want, except maybe those boots. I got to do the job. I'm going to use only one shot, don't want to waste a second cartridge. Ain't going to kill you with it though. Just put you down so you don't fight much while I let the badger here do what he wants with you."

He then let out an evil whistling sound as he pulled the foot-and-a-half long Bowie knife from its scabbard and hissed "meet the badger" as he stuck it in the ground at his feet.

"There's no need to do this you know..."

He picked up his Springfield and took it to his shoulder.

With an empty holster, all I could think to do was close my eyes.

The discharge echoed up and down the length of the gully along with a scream that seemed to come from another world.

The weasel dropped at my feet. I opened my eyes just as his closed.

The Ranger stood at the top of the ridge, chambering another round as he stepped forward to the very edge.

Another round discharged and echoed. The weasel twitched one last time.

"We've been following him for months. It wasn't until they left Abilene that I realized he grew hair and shaved his beard," the Ranger explained, as he made his way down the cut and into the gully. "Carleton tried to ambush me a few miles back, but I made sure he shot my duster when I wasn't in it. You alright?"

"I am just dandy, thank you."

We carried the weasel, a man whose given name was Earl Smudgins, to the top of the break. I helped the Ranger tie him on the saddle of the same horse that already had Carleton on it.

"You want me to help you with that cactus growin' out of your ear?"

With everything else that was going on I forgot about the needles I picked up in my right ear while tumbling down the ditch. Over the years I have learned that the only thing worse than getting into things with needles is pickin' 'em out. If you can see them to work on them, that's one thing. When you can't see them and you just have to feel for 'em, it's worse than when they went in the first place.

"I would certainly appreciate your help in that regard."

The Ranger stepped up beside me and studied the situation.

"Looks like five of them. Three are clean through we'll have to pull them on out. One in your lobe and one in your neck."

He walked over to his horse and started poking around in his saddlebags.

"Yucca, cactus and porkypines...things with points. Could do without all of them," he said.

"Ah", he whispered, celebrating the finding of a couple of pieces of wood in the bag. "I saw this contraption being used by an Apache down near Tombstone." He held it up in front of me so I didn't have to turn my head. They were two pieces of branch that had been whittled down to about little finger size, both notched on one end and tied together with yucca string. When he pinched down on them the untied end squeezed together and when he let up it stuck together for a moment before springing open again. Those damned needles were really starting to smart.

"Sap. That's the secret. Every time I get close to a bleeding pine I put more on. Without it being sticky, it don't work near as well".

He made short order of the needles...not without pain, mind you, but the process was as slick as I had ever seen. He put the contraption back in his bag, produced a small flask that he claimed would help heal the wounds and smeared his damp fingertip across the needle holes. The devil's tongue itself couldn't have hurt more.

"I'm much obliged, sir" I said through clenched teeth while I gathered myself.

"Looks to me like you need a horse."

"Yes, I could really use a horse."

"Neither one of them is going to need one."

"Nope, guess not. Besides, that paint has my saddle on it."

"I'm sure there's an interesting story that goes with that. You will have to tell it some other time though. I need to get back to Abilene. Don't forget your Colt over there in the sage brush. Anything else I can do for you?"

"Mind if I take Carleton's boots if I replace them with mine?"

"Go ahead. Yours look to be in a lot better shape than his, though."

"Yup, they are.   But these are cursed...and the heels are all wrong."

BACK IN THE SADDLE AGAIN

The weight of the world had been lifted from my shoulders. I knew who the men were that were following me, and I knew the man that was following them. I now had a horse under me and was probably a day's ride from catching up with Story's cattle and, hopefully, a job and grub. Can't really say that the Bull Snake had filled the entire void that was once my belly.

I just let the horse find his way along the drive trail and he was happy to just mosey along. The steady, smooth gait made me drowsy, and I guess my saddle still fit my butt well enough to make me at home because I was eventually awakened by a deep voice yelling "Halt, Rider".

I set up straight in the saddle and instinctively reached for my holster. Only thing that kept me from drawing my Colt was that there were 68 sets of eyeballs staring at me.....136, if you count the horses. It appeared that an entire company of mounted Cavalry had somehow managed to sneak up within 20 feet of me while I was alertly guiding my horse toward Nebraska Territory.

"Where would you be riding to, young man?"

"Headed up to Nebraska Territory to seek out Nelson Story's herd in hopes that I can get on with his company and go to Montana," I blurted out, nervously.

"You riding by yourself?"

"Yes Sir."

"I'm Captain Benteen of the 7th Cavalry. We're charged with keeping the peace in this part of the world."

"A true honor to meet you, Captain Benteen" as I instinctively snapped off a salute.

"That behavior would normally come from a military man. You served?"

"For a couple of months down in Louisiana."

"Which side?"

"Union, sir."

"Still going on, both down there and, in the minds of some, up here."

"Yes, sir, that is true enough."

"You hail from hereabouts?"

"Birthed in Arkansas. My father was conscripted to Fort Scott. He went to Mexico and was killed there in September of '47 near Mexico City."

"I was at Scott. What was your father's name?"

"William Graham, sir. He was a lieutenant while he was at Scott."

"I knew him well. Good man. Wondered what had become of him."

"He was promoted in the field in Mexico and died a general. My mother passed shortly after receiving news of father's death...a broken heart, I'm thinking. I was sent to live with Captain Sword and his wife Charlotte at Fort Scott."

"Sword was my commanding officer. I believe I remember you at the Fort. Not one to shy away from adventure or trouble as I recall. I was at Scott until transferred to Ft. Atkinson in Nebraska when I was commissioned. I went back to witness the closing of Fort Scott in 1853. Sad day, that. Oh, well, as they say, 'new day'."

"Yes Sir, I rode through Fort Scott a few years back. All of the buildings on the grounds are now owned by townspeople. Most were well maintained, others not so."

"Not like we did though, right?"

"Certainly not."

"A pleasure to be re-acquainted, sir."

"The pleasure would be mine."

"Now, I am required to advise you that a small group of Pottawatomie braves are causing trouble in the area. They seem most interested in taking horses, particularly shod horses, but they have recently become more aggressive in their manner and their thievery. It would be a good idea to stay alert...and that doesn't mean sleeping in the saddle".

"Yes, sir."

"By the way, the herd you are seeking is about a day's ride north/northwest, out near a little settlement named Imperial. You stay on this track it will take you there. I was told that he had a thousand head in that herd but from what we saw I'd say it's closer to three thousand. Trail boss said they had $10,000 dollars tied up in them steers and they were headed for Bozeman, Montana Territory. Looked to me like they needed more hands.

If it doesn't work out and you are looking for pay, room and board, come seek me out at Fort Atkinson. We're needing good soldiers and since you have some knowledge about what military life is all about, you would have a leg up on others. Recruits that can ride and shoot get paid $8 a month, room and board and medical care."

"I appreciate that information, Captain, I truly do"

"Be safe in your travels, Mr. Graham".

"And in yours, Captain."

With a wave of our hands we went our

own way...he and his company going south and me and my horse working north.

RECOLLECTIONS

With a little pressure on my heels, the spurs put a little more life into my horse. I was hoping I could get to Imperial and get on the Story drive tomorrow. As I rode along I thought about how strange it was to be called by my real name. Since my birth in 1845 I was a Graham for about 18 years. Then there was that unfortunate misunderstanding about my intentions toward a young lady in Lubbock and a brief skirmish that ended in a pretty good brawl, during which somebody, not me, pulled off a round that wounded a deputy. I wasn't the only one getting out of town as fast as I could, but I was sure I was the one that got blamed for the shooting.

I wasn't six miles out of town when Andrew Graham became Clyde Driscoll.

Back at Fort Scott, Andy Graham was known as something of a terror. I was, however, the ward of the Base Commandant. As a result, I had certain liberties that weren't available to enlisted men, junior officers, slaves, contractors or even other people's children. Aside from the regular everyday adventures that were available on the frontier, there were all the things that made a fort work.

I had free rein. In my wanderings I learned baking, horses, laundry, shooting, legal proceedings and imprisonment. I also learned manners and, most importantly, how to read and write. Despite being a hellion I quickly learned that you never repeated anything you heard and, consequently, I was often allowed to be places that afforded even greater insight and adventure. I was on hand to learn of battle strategies, how to judge horses, how to conduct a court martial and even how to brand deserters. Deserters are those who choose to escape the military life. Although I was exempt from the hardships that were everyday occurrences for the enlisted men, I came to understand how difficult life could be as an enlisted man and often wondered why they just didn't disappear into the night and get on with their life.

It was in early July of 1856, at the age of 10, when I came to understand why more men didn't just desert their post. Out of the east came a group of four riders. One a Marshal from Missouri and two were bounty hunters. The fourth was a soldier, a skinny lad named Ewing. I often talked to him about horses as he seemed to understand them. Seemed like he was always on extra duty for something.

Then he made the mistake of stealing a couple of overcoats and selling them so he could buy some whiskey. For weeks he had been in the stockade and forced to stand on the cask for days on end. Evidently, he decided he had been through enough punishment and headed east after using a barrel stave to render the guard unconscious. Most of the soldiers knew better that to go east into Missouri because deserters were held in contempt by most folks...and there was a sizeable reward for capturing a deserter.

Going west was safer......if you didn't take Indians, starvation, prairie fires, desperate ex-slaves and bounty hunters into consideration. South wasn't a good idea either because Kansas was declared a territory in 1854, and more and more settlers had come to the region. It was becoming way too civilized. Towns were springing up everywhere and every one of them had a Sheriff that was always on the lookout for stranger, just in case they were deserters or some other ilk of troublemaker.

North put you directly on a path of

confrontation with several Indian tribes, notably the Miami, Chippewa, Shawnee and Ottawa. Being a lone rider that was unarmed and wearing military dress would most certainly lower your life expectancy appreciably.

Ewing was captured and returned to the Fort. As a deserter he was locked in solitary confinement until he was branded. Deserters would go through life with a "D" on their face or back of their hand according to the proceedings of the court martial. Shame, harassment and, many times, suicide followed. Ewing chose the back of his right hand. That night he was ordered removed from the Fort and he walked away into the darkness.

Unfortunately, the things that led to a soldier's punishment were many and, most would say, the deed that created jail time, keg standing, and rack riding didn't seem to justify the punishment.

I always understood why swearing at officers, fighting, disobedience and desertion were wrong and deserved punishment, but I was also privy to the proceedings when substantial penalties were given for seemingly minor issues. I witnessed severe punishment being ordered for such things as hunting on Indian lands, playing cards with a negro slave, going to sleep on duty and even dumping ashes in the wrong place.

I will always remember the day when three soldiers each received the same isolation punishment...one for shooting at his wife, the other for whipping a laundress and the next for playing "hustle caps", a game that consisted solely of flipping a coin into the air and predicting the outcome.

Even as agonizing as some of the punishment methods were, I couldn't conceive that anything could be so bad as to make a man desert...and I would never, ever, consider doing that, no matter what.

My life at the Fort ended during a tribunal on my 16th birthday when Captain Sword brought forth the fact that I could legally serve in the military. He also pointed out that one, or possibly two, of the daughters of senior officers at the fort had evidently caught my eye and their fathers were concerned that I was giving their daughters just a little too much attention. Captain Sword offered me three choices. Go back east to a military school and come back in two years to enlist as an officer, enlist now or the last...and the one I chose, was to make my way into this world by signing on with a ranch and becoming a drover... I could work cattle while I figured out what I was going to be when I grew up.

My first attempt at herding steers resulted in missing livestock, an embarrassing fall off the saddle while tangled in my own lariat and a sound beating when I started a fight with the Trail Boss because he was poking fun at me in front of the other hands around the campfire...and that was all on my first day in my new profession. Come the next sunrise, I was alone, unemployed and looking for a more fulfilling life, which I was certain could be found in saloons and brothels across Texas.

THE DEMISE OF ANDY GRAHAM

Over the course of the next two years, I wandered about Texas and was given a second education on the streets, trails, bedrooms, saloons and prairies. Then one day I wandered into Lubbock. I had a sense that change was in the air. Now I'm not a big man. In my stocking feet I can stretch to about 5 foot 10 inches. Later on in life, I made 6 foot tall, but that was because I was wearing boots with a #5 Riding Heel. I'm not wide either...My usual 170-pound body is fit but certainly not intimidating.

So, on the morning of the day being considered, I had just left the hotel after a good night's drinking. My horse and I lazily rode toward downtown, looking down each of the side streets and wondering what adventure might be awaiting. I chose one of the avenues and found myself riding through the middle of several very large, very important-looking residences.

From the looks I was getting from those working in the yards and walking on the boardwalks, I just didn't fit into the neighborhood. At one point, a very well-dressed gentleman stopped, placed his hands on his hips and watched as I approached. His gestures advised that I needed to get back on the main street, which he pointed to with a gloved finger.

The message was clear, and I turned at the corner as his finger had directed. While doing so I gave him my most crisp, half-assed salute and my most outlandish, and generous, smile. He clearly was shocked that I should respond in such a manner.

"I hope he is a shopkeeper or a banker and not the Mayor or Sheriff's father", I quietly whispered.

I just turned back onto the dusty main street through town and was on the edge of the red-light district when I spotted a very lovely image of womanhood making her way onto the boardwalk. She appeared to be heading for Gwendolyn's, one of my favorite houses in town.

I matched my horse's speed up to her pace and used my most manly voice to open the conversation, "Good morning, Ma'am. My, aren't you the vision of loveliness all bright and clean and pretty."

"Good morning, Sir. Do we know each other?" queried the beauty.

"No, I haven't the honor. My name is Andy Graham. I am certain, however, that later on you won't be as clean and fresh as you are right now. I'm wondering if I might be the first to share your bed this day?"

While she was processing the words I had just spoken, her expression slowly changed from innocent curiosity to absolute horror. It was as if she had seen a ghost or something equally horrifying. It was precisely at that time I realized she likely wasn't a girl from one of the sporting houses but the child of a local family living in those big, fancy houses. I quickly reined my horse to the other side of the street, jumped out of the saddle and went into the saloon...for a drink, yes, but also because I was certain she wouldn't come into the place.

The saloon was crowded, even this early in the morning. There were drovers that had just arrived and needed to rinse the trail dust out of some very parched throats. There were also drovers that were tossing down their last drink and hoping that they had enough to last for weeks.

I was able to squeeze into a small space at the bar between two very large men. The one on my right accepted the intrusion and turned sideways slightly to let me have a couple of inches of additional space. The one on my left pushed back hard enough that I bumped up against the big guy on my right.   He looked in my direction and belched out "mind your manners". For a moment I was certain he was talking to me, but the fact was that he was talking over my head to the guy on my left.

Almost precisely at that moment I heard a very angry, young female voice say, "That's him, Daddy. The little guy at the bar." I immediately knew I was being singled out and turned, looking to find an exit.

With two very long strides a big fellow wearing a business suit and bowler was upon me. I saw the fist coming but there wasn't anything I could do. I knew I was headed for the floor, even before the full impact of the swing arrived. The punch sent me flying backward into the big guy on my right. Part of his spilled beer found its way down to the floor at the same time I did. With that, the big guy on the right says, "All right, I have had enough."

From floor level I see Mr. Suit step forward and give a shrug with open palms at his side...a sort of "what else could I do?" look that went away the minute the Big Right Guy's fist spun Mr. Suit to the floor. Big Left Guy mimicked "mind your manners" and Big Right Guy delivered a left cross that barely made Big Left Guy flinch, and the rest, as they say, is history.

The lovely lady that was responsible for this whole melee ran toward her father but was immediately caught up in the bodies and punches and beer and breaking glass. I crawled over to her, picked her up and got her to the edge of the room. With my right arm around her waist and my left over her shoulder I was fending off whatever was coming that way. She looked at me and recognized that I was the instigator. Right at that moment, I heard the gunshot. Most of those fighting stopped as the Deputy fell to the floor.

The saloon emptied out instantly, with people going out doors, windows and stairways. I joined the throng as I didn't see any opportunity to have a meaningful conversation with the young lady at that particular moment. Since I was planning on leaving Lubbock anyway, I didn't see any need to hang around for extended goodbyes. I was on the open prairie in less than five minutes.

It suddenly occurred to me that the little lady knew my name. That was not a good thing. I knew that she was aware that I didn't pull the trigger, but this didn't seem like a good time to go back and have that conversation. I decided to get back to her later on to see if I could clear my name.

About six miles out of Lubbock, for all intents and purposes, Andy Graham disappeared from this earth. In his saddle was one Clyde Driscoll. Clyde spurred his paint to put more distance between himself and an angry group of upstanding citizens and lawmen in Lubbock.

CLYDE DRISCOLL

Clyde Driscoll was a good name, a safe name.   Only a handful of people would recall it and they would have to live around Deerfield, Missouri. It was unlikely Clyde would be anywhere near there.

Andy was only about two years old when he left Deerfield, he remembered the name as it was the very first thing that Andy learned to say. "Cleyedrisco" was the word he would utter every time he saw his friend from down the road. When he was just barely four years old Clyde came down with a fever late one evening and died early the next day. Aside from possibly being etched into a stone in the Deerfield Cemetery, there was no Clyde Driscoll until the very moment Andy went missing.

***

I decided it was best to work some other trails for the next couple of years.

I had been on so many drives on the Chisholm that it was like a hometown. I knew every creek, watering hole and saloon on both routes. When you signed on in San

Antonio you picked your route...the Ellsworth spur or the Abilene route. Both ran the same trail until you cleared Texas and then the Ellsworth went more west, and the Abilene went east across the Indian Territory that some called Oklahoma.

The Goodnight-Loving, which I had done a couple of times, was a little more challenging for both stock and rider. It started out in San Angelo, Texas, veered west and ended in Cheyenne.

Then there was the so-called Western Trail from Bandera, Texas to Ogallala, Nebraska Territory. Some of Nelson Story's herd went up that way and then joined with the group that went up the Chisholm, on the Abilene side.

Probably the safest route for me was going to be the Shawnee Trail that ran from deep in the south of Texas to Sedalia, Missouri. I didn't want to double back into trouble, so I finally decided to cut west and run into one of the Goodnight-Loving drives. Once they got into Cheyenne, I could sign on as a hand with the railroad and get over to Missouri without attracting much attention...and that's what put me in Sedalia, Missouri a couple of months later, just in time for winter...and what a winter it was.

I sold my horse in Cheyenne, wrapped

up the rest of my gear in a blanket and tossed it in a cattle car heading for what I thought was going to be warmer than the high plains. As it turned out, Old Man Winter was being unkind to Nebraska, Kansas and Missouri. Drives weren't leaving Texas. Drives that were underway were stalled and animals of all kinds were dying for lack of food and water or were freezing in their tracks.

I bought a new horse in Sedalia, with the plan being to go over to St. Joseph where it was reported the temperatures were much more civil. Upon arrival, I found winter to be there too. My second night in town, I talked with a trapper that had just come in from Nebraska and he was sharing a tragic story with anybody that would listen. Fort Atkinson was without most everything that could be used to treat or prevent scurvy or diarrhea. Virtually every fort relied on vegetables and vinegar to treat those diseases. Reports were coming in that as many as 150 men had perished from the diseases or complications associated with the two curses.

Their stores depleted and stock either dead or dying, the Fort was under siege by nature. I talked to a couple of other drovers that were waiting out the winter and we hatched a plan to take a train to as close as we could get to Fort Riley or Fort Leavenworth and then carry stores to Fort Atkinson.

At the station we were told that trains hadn't gone north or west out of St. Joseph for nearly three weeks. The Stationmaster said he heard that the grain-fed horses of the 7th Cavalry were going to be pressed into service, supported by the mules that transport the grains. They would follow the railroad beds to get to the nearest place where the necessary food might be available...Fort Leavenworth, Kansas.

Later we learned that the troops had to turn back the second day of what was planned as a four-day ride. The ride was terrible, certainly, but they turned back because the people in virtually every town in the region were running dangerously low on food. There was nothing they could do except possibly seize whatever food was available in each town. That would be putting the residents in peril and that was an option that would not be considered.

Most all of us felt helpless under the circumstances but there was nothing we could do.

The wind, snow and freezing temperatures continued for another month and a half. From what we were hearing, Fort

Atkinson would have to sacrifice cattle and horses to survive and, ultimately, what might save the remaining troops from starving or sickness, would be the coming of spring and the arrival of wild onions.

For one of the almost two months, I was being held captive by Mother Nature, I was immersed in memories. For the next month I spent time evaluating options for my future.

TAKING BENTEEN'S OFFER

With spring came a return to a more normal existence in the cow and railroad towns. Steers started moving north again and the backlog of other materials was steadily decreasing as time went on.

The thought of getting on a drive and having to fight mud, swollen creeks and rivers while sleeping in puddles of melted snow was something I found I wasn't willing to sign on for. Then, one morning in April, I mounted my new horse, crossed the Missouri and headed for Fort Atkinson, Nebraska Territory. I figured that my skills with horses, rifles and pistols I should be able to enlist in the Cavalry in short order. If Atkinson had lost more than 150 men over the winter, they would need people with a background like mine.

If I had been smart, I would have stayed on the east side of the Missouri because the further you went west, the more muck and mire you encountered. I finally altered my course to go through Lincoln and then northeast to get to Atkinson. What normally would have been a two-week adventure became a four-week study in survival, battling weather and avoiding Indians.

The treaties that were in place throughout the west were failing and there was general discontent among Indians and the US government alike. The Manifest Destiny that explained the gluttony and greed of politicians and settlers opened every door to mistreatment of the tribes. As a result, many of the tribes, either in their entirety or as smaller groups of warriors began taking back the lands from which they were forced.

Between daily thunderstorms, unceasing winds and continual surveillance by groups of 10-20 Indians, I was beginning to think my decision was a bad one...and once I arrived at Fort Atkinson, I was certain of it. This is the middle of the northern Great Plains. You can see for miles in any direction...but there is no need to because there is nothing to see. Since that was the case, it wasn't hard for me to find the Fort and the Fort to find me.

As I approached, four riders in uniform came out at a trot to meet me.

"Halt Rider."

"Yes Sir."

"Your name and purpose here".

Now I was in a tough spot. Was I Andy Graham or Clyde Driscoll? If I wanted

Captain Benteen's influence, I had to be Graham. If I wanted continuing anonymity, I had to be Driscoll. Graham was probably wanted and being pursued by the Texas Rangers. Driscoll wasn't.

"Sir, what is your name and purpose," he almost screamed.

"Driscoll, Sir. Clyde Driscoll. I'm requesting enlistment."

Three of the riders gave each other a startled look while the Lieutenant that questioned me kept his eyes on mine.

"Do you come with references?" asked the Lieutenant.

"Only that I have a good friend of General Benteen's that will recommend me."

"General Benteen is no longer in command here."

"Can I ask where General Benteen is stationed?"

"That information is not available to you."

"Can I ask why?"

"Regulations from the general in command."

"May I meet the general in command so that I might apply for enlistment?"

"You will be required to surrender all firearms in your possession before entering."

"If that is the regulation, I will comply."

"You will be required to surrender your

horse and enter on foot."

"I'm not sure I under.........."

"Those are the conditions for entry."

"So be it, then."

I put my Colt in my saddlebags and walked into the Fort. I wasn't ready for the appearance of the Fort as it was not being maintained or in order. The few horses that I saw were barely able to walk and the soldiers appeared to be much in the same state.

"Wait here, while I prepare some documents for you."

I didn't expect a hero's welcome, but I didn't expect to be placed under what was amounting to house arrest either. I was wondering if this was going to be the opportunity that I thought it was going to be.

"Sign here," ordered the Lieutenant, striding out of the Commandant's Office.

"What am I being asked to sign?"

"Your enlistment papers."

COMPARING FORT SCOTT AND FORT ATKINSON

Coming from the experience at Fort Scott I was looking forward to the lodging and food at Fort Atkinson, after all, this was a much larger fort, and it was responsible for a much larger area than Scott was. Upon entering the Commandant's Office, I was surprised to see a captain behind the desk.

"Good day, Sir." I said, while snapping off a very crisp salute.

"At ease, soldier".

"No return salute. General Sword would have had this man in the stockade for months if he were in charge."

"I am Captain Garrity. I am temporarily in charge of Fort Atkinson. This fort will soon come under the command of General George Custer of Fort Riley, Kansas. General Custer will be arriving in Fort Riley in the very near future and will appoint a commander."

I was soon placed with the same Lieutenant that had prevented me from entering the Fort. He remained very staunch and proper, even when he introduced me to the privates in my soon-to-be-home. Two uniforms were brought to me. Both were showing considerable wear, and both needed laundered. I settled into the barracks and began to re-acquaint myself with the life of a cavalryman. I was particularly looking forward to the dinner meal as my stomach was thinking about digesting itself. The Lieutenant stepped into my barracks, and I jumped up and saluted.

"Sir."

"It's good to see somebody that understands the need for propriety," he said while woefully looking around at the other men in the room. There wasn't any sense of hostility but there wasn't any sense of military courtesies either.

"Driscoll, I have assigned you to the kitchen to see if you can do something to make our fare more appealing and healthier." As he left the room he muttered "Please see what miracles you can work."

I saluted to his back as he already turned and stepped out of the door. When I asked if someone would direct me to the kitchen, one of the older soldiers pointed me in the general direction of a building that, evidently, was shared with the laundry.

Pointed wasn't actually correct. It was more of a closed-fist gesture as the thumb and index finger of the single glove that he was wearing were not filled with digits.

"If you don't mind, how did you lose your finger and thumb?"

"Accident and a serious condition required their amputation", he replied in an unusually frank and well-practiced monotone.

I walked toward the kitchen and could smell it from 20 yards away. Not an aroma...an odor. At Fort Scott the kitchen was almost as clean as the hospital. Here, it looked more like a slaughter pen. Pieces of rotting meat lying on the counters and pots, pans, utensils were all scattered about right where they were used for the last meal...which appeared to be a skinny antelope judging from the carcass lying on the floor. The only bread that was in sight was small chunks that were only a few hours from being petrified. Nothing in the oven and nothing edible on the worktable...and it was only two hours to evening mess.

At Scott the meals were certainly not fancy, but they met Army requirements and we, many times, did something different to dress up the fare. Meals consisted of rice soup with dried vegetables, a small piece of boiled beef, a small piece of bread and sometimes we made bean soup with some boiled salt pork and one or two boiled potatoes in it. The men at Scott knew we had to work with what we had. Staples included salt beef, salt pork, beans, rice, flour and coffee...none of which I could find in the stores at Atkinson. I was rummaging around in the building looking in every nook and cranny for something that could be prepared for a meal. Nothing!

Just as I was about to head over to the Commander's Office, a negro woman peeked around the doorway of the kitchen, "What you doin' makin' all that noise in here?" she shrieked.

"I'm trying to do my job but there isn't anything in here to work with," I explained.

"Well then you should come ask me what to do 'stead of throwin' things around."

"Let's start with introductions. I'm Private Driscoll. Who are you?"

"Louisa. Louisa the laundress."

"Louisa. Good name."

"Where do Private Driscoll come from?"

"Little bit of everywhere, Louisa. Most of my army experience is from Fort Scott in Kansas Territory."

"Why dat fort been closed for many years. You join the army when you was six?"

"Younger than that."...and that allowed me to tell her my story, right up to the point where the Commanding Officer encouraged me to find some direction in my life.

"Well, Lawdie, Private Driscoll. What you gonna do to straighten up this Fort. It is a mess."

"Well, yes, it is...but let's start with just finding something to eat."

"I got's all the vittles over on my side. If I left them over here, the soldiers would steal what the mice and rats didn't take."

....and that allowed me to put something edible on the table at mess that night.

Later that night I was cleaning up the kitchen, something that hadn't been done in weeks. I was just about finished with the first go-round when the corporal that had pointed out where the kitchen was, peeked around the corner of the door.

"Come in, Corporal", I snapped off a salute.

That flustered the gentleman, who was decidedly older than anybody else on the fort. He returned the salute, with thumb and index finger on that one glove flapping around and then hanging limp.

"Don't see much saluting going on around here, do you?" I asked.

"No. Not much. When I was young and

in the army it was..." and then his words trailed off into silence. "Anyway, not important, I have guard duty tonight and wondered why the lamp was still lit. I also wanted to thank you for putting some food on the table that I could eat without worrying about having to vomit later tonight."

"Well, thank you for the kind words, at least I think they were kind."

"Certainly so."

"So, Corporal, what is your name?"

"Corporal Ewing."

"You're obviously much older than everybody else here...old enough that I'm surprised you are still in the Army."

"Army is my life. Would rather it had been in some other part of the west but at least here I get, most times, my nine dollars a month, a place to lay my head, some food and medical care when we got somebody here to administer it".

"Where were you before you came up here?"

"Started in a place that isn't any more. Made some bad decisions and was out of the army for 12 years until I came up here and enlisted." I watched as his eyes welled up with tears, "Yes. Bad decisions."

"Won't you tell me what happened to your hand?"

"These days, nobody but me knows what happened. Nobody asks. Why do you want to know?"

"I've always been curious and fascinated with medical treatments. Will you show me?"

His hands started trembling as he pulled the single glove off of his right hand. Once it was removed I could clearly see scar tissue in the shape of a "D".

"You are a deserter! What? How?" I stammered.

"Needed a drink. Stole to get money. Got caught and punished. Lost my thumb and finger because of an infection from the burn. I had to cut them off when they turned black."

"Where did you go after Fort Scott?"

"FORT SCOTT? How did you know this was from Fort Scott?"

"I'm Andy Graham."

"Andy Graham! Little Andy Graham? My goodness-gracious-sakes-alive. But you said your name was Driscoll."

"Now I'll tell you my story..."

GIVING LIFE TO A FORT

While Fort Scott was always gleaming white as a result of frequent whitewashings, Atkinson was faded gray. Nothing was going to get better until there were enough bodies to staff a fully functioning fort.

I felt at home in the kitchen as I spent a considerable amount of time there as a youngster. The compliments kept coming as meals were regular and hardy. A kitchen in a fort is supposed to receive daily inspections by both the Commanding Officer and the Charge Officer. I was certain that nothing had been done in that regard for months.

"Hain't been none in most a full year," said Louisa, "not since Benteen take his troops."

"How come I never hear a bugler?"

"Dey died during the winter. Nobody know how to blow one of 'dem."

"Where are the horses?"

"In da stable, standin' der."

"I've been here for two weeks and I haven't seen a single mounted soldier except for that patrol that goes out to meet people. Do you know why that is?"

"Workin' horses takes mo' care and mo' feed. They ain't nobody that knows how to take care of 'em."

"What about Ewing? He's good with horses."

"Nobody thinks he kin ride or rope 'cuz of his hands. Can't shoot 'cuz the same."

"That's nonsense...maybe he can't just because he doesn't want to."

"I jus' do laundry. I don't pay no 'tension to those things."

"You know everything that goes on is this fort, Louisa, you can't deny that."

She turned and headed for the door. "Deny, I can. Nobody pays 'tension to the little nigger woman...and that's the way it needs to be."

I went out to find Ewing. He was on the far side of what used to be the Parade Grounds.

"Corporal Ewing, can I have a word with you?" I yelled as I walked.

My stride must have given my attitude away.

"Yes, Private Driscoll, you can." OK. Now we're making progress. Ewing is pulling rank on me. It's about time.

"Sir, given that you are accomplished

horseman, why aren't you in charge of getting the Fort's horses back to health and ready for service?"

"Private, nobody ever asked me to do so."

"Do you mind if I ask why you haven't volunteered for that duty?"

"Private, only idiots would volunteer for that duty at this fort. The horses have been standing in the same stalls for months. Their hooves need trimming, shoes set. They can hardly walk, let alone trot or run. Why would I want that responsibility?"

"Because it was widely known you were the best horse man in the Army while at Fort Scott."

"Fort Scott is gone, only a memory...and not a good one, either. You and I both need to remember that we were never there, would you not agree?

"Given your situation, how did you get enlisted?"

"Nobody asked about my history. They wanted to know about my hand. When they asked what happened, I gave them my 'accident' and amputation story. When they asked what I could do with it, I told them anything they can do. Nobody ever asked to see it...until you. As long as I keep a glove on it, nobody will ever know of my transgressions."

"Ewing, I'll make you a deal...."

"Corporal Ewing, Private."

"My apologies, Corporal. I'll train some men to take care of the farrier's duties. They can feed and muck the stalls according to accepted military practice. You just need to get the horses fit and re-train them in military function."

"You will never get Captain Garrity and the Lieutenant to go along with that. If you do, I'll take your deal."

Garrity and the Lieutenant were willing to go along with anything being proposed as long as it didn't mean more work for them.

The next day, the horses were taken from their stalls and brought out into the daylight for the first time in months. The Officers horses had been well-fed and taken care of. The rest of those that survived the winter were in sad, sad shape. Ewing had to wonder why he had taken on such an arduous task.

Every aspect of function was lacking. I found the armory unlocked but it didn't make any difference as the rifles and other weapons were missing. Ammunition wasn't to be found either.

I walked into the Laundry at a full stride, "Ok, Louisa, where are the guns and ammunition?"

"Under the floor," she said, without even looking up from her mending.

"Why on earth..."?

"Cuz if I don't have 'em, dey go away."

"I'll bring some men over and we'll get that stuff back in the Armory. Do you know if the gunpowder is still in the powder magazines?"

"Yep."

"Yep, you know or yep, it is?"

"Yep."

"Louisa, quit playing games with me."

"When did you get charge of dis place."

"Ok. That's an appropriate question. I'm going to go as far as I can on getting this place back in order before I get reprimanded. This is a travesty."

"Your big words goin' to weigh heavy on your shoulders sometime soon. Big changes comin'."

"What do you hear? Are we going to have a new Commanding Officer?"

"Custer has a man he wants here...another man who will become the next Custer."

"What does that mean?"

"Custer sent a Commander away. Got a man named Reno. Reno never got here 'cuz Custer put him some other place. The man was a drinker. Garrity put here to sit while

Custer decides what he wants. May close dis fort."

That was a jolt. The possibility of closing the fort had never crossed my mind. Given the situation with all of the Indian unrest and the size of the area that it covered, I couldn't imagine that would happen. I had to remember that if I was to be transferred to another fort, I might have to provide more information than I could. It was worth worrying about.

"Well, we need to get this fort to look and work like a fort. Is there powder in the magazines?"

Yep. My locks on 'em though."

"What? WHY?"

"Powder and cannons."

"CANNONS? We have cannons here? HOW?"

"Custer brung 'em from someplace for some reason. I rolled 'em over one night when I saw no guard."

Louisa went over to a bag of soap, burrowed her hand down until she was up to her elbow. Wiggling her hand around until she stopped, smiled and lifted the key out of the powder.

"Who knew about this?"

"Corporal Ewing".

"Anybody else?"

"Couple dead men. One dried and died. One froze."

"Ok. We have a lot to do.   Thanks for looking after the fort for this last year."

"This is home. Guard your home."

LOOKING LIKE A FORT

We were making giant strides. Even the most insolent and disinterested were stepping forward and getting involved. Almost everybody, it seemed, except Captain Garrity. We re-established and secured the Arsenal and Armory. Louisa's cannons turned out to be two 6-pound Mountain Howitzers and two 12-Pound Lightweight Mountain Howitzers that were once assigned to the Dragoons in the 1840s and early 1850s.

The 6-pounders were used for two reasons. The first was to scare the Indians and the second was for rounds to be fired at special occasions. I often had the chance to discharge them at Fort Scott, so I knew them well.

The 12-pounders were a different thing. With a five-degree elevation and an eight-ounce powder charge a 12-pound round could be fired about 900 yards. They truly were a weapon. Our soldiers at Fort Scott could offload the three horses or mules that were transporting the howitzers, have them reassembled and fired in one minute. A good company could turn the tide of a battle with the presence of the 12-pound howitzers.

The appearance of the howitzers changed the way the soldiers saw themselves. They were no longer disinterested caretakers of a bunch of run-down buildings, there were truly soldiers. Men that had not ridden a horse, discharged a firearm or drawn a sword were now dressing to come to mess and practicing drills.

Most impressive, however, was the men on horseback. They had selected "their" horses and were taking care of them. Saddles, bridles and all leather gear were shining in the sun. The horses had re-learned all of their battle gaits and were excelling at close order drills.

Cavalry men started acting like rank actually mattered and salutes were the order of the day, and they were expected to be returned. On those rare occasions where a new recruit appeared, he was welcomed and befriended.

The Lieutenant had been watching, very closely, the progress of all elements. He was, indeed, officer material as he chose not to meddle in what was happening.

Garrity remained a mystery. The

Lieutenant would often go into the Commanding Officer's office and was summoned to the Captain's Quarters every couple of days, but Garrity was never on rounds or in contact with the men.

....and then, the unexpected happened. Two men took it upon themselves to learn how to blow the bugle. For the first couple of days, terrible noises were heard throughout the surrounding hills but on the third the men were awakened to Reveille. That was the signal everyone responded to...there were soldiers in the fort once again.

TRANSITION

Just after the noon meal on a Thursday in September, the bugler signaled that we had visitors, and it had to be important people because it looked like hundreds of mounted cavalrymen were coming in...under the 7th Cavalry flag. Our still depleted companies stood at attention while the troops arrived and established themselves on the now-green parade grounds. Custer, who had just assumed his position at Fort Riley, Kansas, had issued orders to not only replace Captain Garrity but also evaluate whether Fort Atkinson should be de-commissioned and closed.

A brief meeting was held in the Court Martial Office which was located adjacent to the Commandant's Office. Elsewhere about a dozen lieutenants and a couple of first sergeants walked throughout the Fort evaluating condition and readiness. It became evident they were very surprised and pleased with the situation that existed there, particularly since the winter that just passed was still on everybody's mind. The Lieutenant was called into the room and walked out as a captain.

Captain Garrity came out in chains. He looked gaunt and tired, with little evidence of will to live. He was placed on a buckboard for his trip to Fort Riley. With little ceremony, the troops mounted up, fell into columns and headed back into the prairie.

The new captain ordered an assembly, and the bugler called the troops. The Captain explained that he would be in charge of the Fort until Major Reno arrived to take over the Commandant's position. He then complimented everybody for the work that had recently been done and reported that the tribunal that performed the review would make the recommendation to retain Fort Atkinson. The troops of Fort Atkinson heard the message and read it correctly. They departed the assembly with a great deal of pride and purpose.

DISCOVERY

The Saturday following the visit, Corporal Ewing and I were evaluating the animal stock with the purpose of finding out what needed to be procured to get us through the next winter.

The Captain rode up to us on his newly assigned black. In most forts, companies would choose a color of horse that would become their trademark. Atkinson did not have enough stock to allow for that, but the Captain made it known all senior officers would be riding black horses.

As the Captain dismounted, I had that old sense something was awry.

"Corporal Ewing, in reviewing the comments from the recent tribunal, I noted that one of the few exceptions noted on the inspection was that you were out of uniform as a result of not only wearing gloves but also wearing only one such glove. I've observed that to be the case since my arrival but chose to disregard it as it doesn't seem to prevent you from doing your work. Can you explain the reason behind your use of one glove?"

"Yes sir. As a result of an accident, I got

an infection that required the amputation of my thumb and finger. My hand is disfigured. It makes people uncomfortable, so I wear the glove."

"Corporal, let me see your hand."

"I would rather not sir."

"It doesn't make any difference what you would rather not. Remove the glove."

Ewing slowly worked the glove off and extended his hand to the Captain palm up.

The Captain looked intently at the scar created by the amputation and appeared to understand the need for the glove.

"I see, Corporal. Let's consider this to be a closed issue."

He turned to get back on his horse when he realized Ewing had not saluted. He turned around and asked if there was a reason he was not saluted upon departure. Ewing did his best to turn away enough that the scar tissue would not present the tell-tale D and he saluted.

The Captain's face fell into a grimace, and he grabbed Ewing's arm, forcing Ewing to turn the back of his hand upward.

"A deserter. You are a deserter. Yet you have been here for years. How unfortunate."

It seemed that he was trying to figure out how to overlook the situation but then he shook his head, and I knew what was coming.

"Guard, come here," he yelled across the parade grounds.

Two responded, as they should.

"Put Corporal Ewing in the stockade. I will prepare the charges".

With that, the Captain mounted his horse and hurried himself away from a very difficult situation.

PLEADING THE CASE AND REQUESTING A PARDON

I stood near the stable, trying to make sense of what had just happened. Ewing had been a good soldier for as long as he had been in Atkinson. Further, he was instrumental in restoring the facility to not only a working fort, but a showcase that even the 7th Cavalry officers had complimented.

I knocked on the Commandant's Office door and heard "enter".

As soon as I entered the office I could feel a storm brewing.

"What is it, Private?"

"Sir, I would like to speak in support of Corporal Ewing. He is a good soldier."

"Unfortunately, you do not determine who is a good soldier on this post. I do."

"Yes sir, I was just hoping to be able to tell you of the many things that he did in rebuilding the fort."

"I am well aware. Speaking of being aware, I am also aware of the fact that you are a private...a private that has been establishing priorities and making assignments without permission to do so."

"Yes sir, I was only doing what I felt needed to be done for the well-being of the fort."

"That is clearly my responsibility. Now, understand this. I intend to, once again, court martial Corporal Ewing and he will be removed from the fort".

"Sir, that is going to..."

We were both startled by the report. Both of us immediately recognized the sound of a Colt 45.

As we ran to the door, we heard one of the guards yell "Ewing done killed hisself".

I turned to the Captain, "will you approve a pardon?"

"Yes," he said, lowering his head. "Yes, I will."

CLOUDS ON THE HORIZON

Ewing's suicide cast a black cloud over the fort.

The official report recorded it as an accidental discharge of a firearm resulting in death. There would be an inquiry, but it would be internal and the records would forever reflect the words penned by the Commandant. Three days after "the incident", Corporal Leland left the fort very early in the morning, riding hard on the Captain's black horse. Leland was a former Pony Express rider. He was as smooth in the saddle as any man. His marksmanship was something that would be talked about for years in the Cavalry and it didn't make any difference if it was a pistol or rifle, his aim was always true.

The only reason I saw him head out before daybreak is that I had not been able to sleep, and I had gone to the bakery to make some bread for the coming meal.

As I listened to the hoof beats pick up cadence and then disappear into the morning noises, I wondered what would motivate the Captain to give up his horse. It was recognized as being most fit in the unit and, without doubt, it had incredible endurance. I came to the conclusion that Leland was assigned to be a courier and was heading someplace distant with an urgent message...probably Fort Riley, headquarters of the 7th.

After breakfast I walked over to the Laundry, planning on talking with Louisa about the event, "Good morning," I said, quietly, still invisible around the corner of the door.

"Why you hidin' out dere?"

"I'm not hiding. Just wanted to make sure you were here and willing to talk to me."

"I'm always here. Got no place else to be. I 'magine you feelin' like you pull da trigger."

"No. Well, I don't know. I mean he laid low so well for so many years until I came along."

"An you was his friend."

"Yes. But that might be what got him caught and why he killed himself."

"Many things an' many years did dat. Not you."

"It's going to be on my mind for quite a while."

"You ain't lone in dat".

Laundresses in a fort were in an unusual position. There was one Laundress per barrack, and they were many times the linchpins that kept things together. They were salaried employees that were most often paid by the piece, were given one ration per day and medical care was provided. They would always be paid, even if there weren't enough funds to pay the soldiers. Their function included much more than washing, ironing and sewing and they were entitled to their own quarters, which most often also housed the laundry equipment.

"You know, you got things to pay 'tension to."

"What."

"The Captain, he watchin' you. He's somethin' in mind. Don' know what, but somethin'."

"Well, if you hear something, please let me know. I don't need any trouble."

"Nobody need trouble".

I returned to my bunk and put on my uniform as we were expecting to have a parade review.

My bunk was one of six in the room. Most times two soldiers would share the same bunk, especially in winter when warmth was hard to come by. Since we were still undermanned most of us had our own bunk. Certainly not fancy, just a wood slab, with a   fabric pocket as a mattress, stuffed with prairie grass that we swapped out a couple times a year. Not much, but better than the floor.

I asked Llewelyn, another private, if he would help me move a rick of wood from the edge of the fort to closer to the Bakery. His response told me I was being watched.

"You'll have to get permission from the Sergeant".

"Why?"

"We have to follow protocol from now on."

"For moving wood?"

"For anything".

"Never mind.   More trouble to get permission than to move the wood."

"So that's the way it's going to be," I said to myself, "No more 'get it done'. Now it's 'can I do it, please?'".

That's going to slow things down and winter isn't that far away.

Three days later, the bugler signaled we had visitors.

A full company from Fort Riley had arrived, led by Leland on the Captains black horse. We soon learned they were to be permanently stationed at Atkinson.   I recognized immediately that things were going to hell in a handbasket now.

Life at a fort required that there was a distinct difference and separation between Officers, Non-Commissioned Officers and Privates. It just wasn't acceptable to have any social interaction between the stations and the non-commissioned officers maintaining separation from the Privates was always a challenge...a powder keg named privilege. A company consists of 50 Privates divided into 4 squads, 2 buglers, a farrier/blacksmith, 2 - 4 Lieutenants, a Captain, 4 Sergeants and 4 Corporals. Atkinson did not have space for a full Company.

When they arrived, it was obvious they were in dismay over the location and reputation of the Fort. They came from Riley. They had the best compound and the best of quarters there. Their horses were exceptionally fit and well cared for. The same could be said for the soldiers. Animosity and jealousy immediately settled over Fort Atkinson...every person stationed here prior to the arrival of the Riley troops felt threatened. Every new arrival wondered what the hell they had done to deserve such an assignment. That circumstance, bad as it was, was nothing compared to the reality that there was not enough food or housing ...for neither man nor beast.

Following dismissal from the parade call, I made my way over to the Laundry, "You knew this was coming, didn't you?"

"Ah did. Ah was asked to find mo' Laundresses. Ah been takin' care a three barracks but can't do seven."

"Did you find more."

"I din't. Nobody aroun' to work."

"Louisa, winter is just weeks away and we can't do this."

"Ah know."

"I have to talk with the Commandant about this."

"Ah wouldn't."

"Why?"

"That like sayin' 'Sir, you ain't smart enuff to see dis so I'll tell you."

"I see. You're right. So, what are we going to do?"

"Git ready to suffer."

I walked out of the Laundry, intent on saying my peace to the Captain but Louisa's words of warning kept echoing in my ears.

"OK, Graham, put it out of your mind. GRAHAM? Where did that come from?"

"Private! Come HERE." The order carried such urgency that I spun hard to determine what dire emergency had arisen. "My horse is lathered from the ride. Rinse him down and cool him off before putting him in his stall," ordered a newly arrived lieutenant.

"Sir", I offered, "I will take your horse to the stable to find out who is on duty there today. I expect that they will only be able to wipe your horse down as water is hard to come by out here and we are under orders not to use water outside of our basic daily requirements."

"Whose orders?"

"Commandant's, Sir".

"Well, we'll see about that. Go then."

"Yes, Sir!"

"So, that's the way it's going to be. This is not a good thing. Not at all."

DEPARTURE

Chaos! That's the only way to describe the next few days.

Every one of the new arrivals acted like they were graduates of West Point. Questioned authority and seniority were the order of the day and thinly veiled threats were common in most every conversation. In effect, I was hiding in the kitchen. Doing so was justified because we were not ready for feeding an additional 65 soldiers, most of which felt they could demand extra rations. At least three different meals almost ended up in a brawl when demands were made either to Mess Staff or to other soldiers.

Four days into the siege, I was taking some apron coverings over to the Laundry when I was stopped by a new sergeant who told me I would have to return later. When I asked why, he pulled rank and said it was not any of my business.

Four straight 18-hour days had taken their toll on my patience, "I don't have time to return. Take these to the laundry whenever you see it appropriate." I said.

I dropped the aprons on the ground at

the feet of the Sergeant and turned to walk away. I felt the muzzle of the Springfield push against the nape of my neck. Just before I felt the butt of the gunstock hit me, I heard "Smart-assed school kid, is that it?"

With the world spinning around I tried to get to my knees, only to feel his boot in my ribs.

"You stop dat!" came Louisa's screeching voice from across the parade grounds.

"Halt Negro!" ...and a shot rang out.

I gathered my senses enough to see Louisa fall to the ground and attempt to get up, only to collapse again. Everybody from the old fort ran to Louisa's side, even the Commandant. Tense moments followed. The anxiety created by the arrivals was close to boiling over.

The Commandant yelled, "Stand Down"...and then again, "Stand Down, NOW!"

Slowly all arms were lowered. Louisa's moaning turned into sobbing and pleas for help. She was picked up and taken to the hospital, which seemed like the thing to do but it was of little good as there was no medical care available. The newly arrived farrier/blacksmith was summoned and went to do what he could to help Louisa. Had

Ewing been here, Louisa would have suffered much less than she did before she died of a shot through her lungs.

"Another person that died as a result of being my friend."

I was completely overtaken with remorse. I went into the stable and sobbed uncontrollably.

I would hear later that Louisa was evidently being questioned as to why she had not been able to secure the services of additional laundresses. She reported that this wasn't Kansas Territory and there aren't many settlers up in these parts, let alone a white woman that wanted to be a laundress in a fort. She went on to say that emancipated slaves were staying south of this region because of the unfriendly weather and that squaws were not a possibility for many reasons, one of which was their distrust of white man in general and the Cavalry in particular.

Her thorough explanation was evidently not well received, and she was being escorted to the Commandant's office when she was murdered while trying to help me. After a brief tribunal, it was determined that I was responsible for the confrontation with the sergeant. I was required to spend three days standing on a barrel, which I much preferred to sitting across a sawbuck. I was greatly relieved when the Commandant excused two days of the punishment...a ruling that was not well received by the newcomers.

The corporal that shot Louisa was from Alabama and had deep hatred for negroes. Everybody in the company knew of his bent in that regard. Even though she was unable to move quickly after all of her years of working bent-over, he simply chose not to catch-up with her but rather stop, raise his rifle and pull off the round that killed her while she was "fleeing" and "interfering with an arrest". For this grave injustice, the murderer was given three weeks in solitary confinement and was demoted too private. I was quickly losing my faith in my commanding officer, the cavalry and the future of Fort Atkinson.

The day on the cask allowed me to clearly consider my options. Late in the day, while the duty guard was in the Brig providing drinking water for other prisoners, the Sergeant that had attacked me came walking toward me with an ax-handle at his side. I was aware that any disturbance, even falling off the cask, would result in yet another day to be added onto the punishment. I decided not to call for the guard, hoping that he would return to his post on the porch of the guard house before the Sergeant got to me.

The Sergeant glanced around the Parade Ground to make certain that nobody was watching and then took a hard swing of the handle, intending to hit me across my back. I let out the loudest yell I could muster. Just before the wood hit me I forced my tired, aching legs to jump and the flat of the handle came square across my butt. I ended up on the ground because as he hit me I came down on the edge of the cask, which then spun out from under me, dropping me flat on the back of my shoulders and knocking the air out of me.

To my surprise, the Sergeant began yelling. "Help in the Guard House, help in the Guard House!"

Soon there were several soldiers looking down at me while I was lying on the ground. The Sergeant was quick to report that he had observed me fall asleep and I had collapsed on the cask, hurting my back. There were a number of glances between soldiers that indicated they didn't exactly believe what they were being told. Some of the "old" soldiers came over to get me standing up but the Sergeant was yelling at them that they shouldn't do that because I probably had a broken back and shouldn't be moved. Once on my feet I was able to disprove the theory of the broken back. That news truly seemed to distress the Sergeant.

I was taken out of the chains and carried to the hospital. They almost certainly placed me on the same bed that Louisa died on less than 24 hours ago. In the middle of the night there was a ruckus with considerable shouting in the barracks. About two hours after that quieted down I was certain that I could hear a horse snort as it was being led behind the hospital and then off the post. Late the next day, somebody reported that Private Llewelyn failed to report to the stable and was nowhere to be found on the grounds. He was, therefore, assumed to be a deserter.

There had evidently been some concern about desertion because the crowding, coming winter, talk of little food and the remote nature of the outpost. The situation had both old and new hands concerned. A squad of the new soldiers was put on notice to pursue deserters until they were either killed or captured and returned to the fort for trial.

Llewelyn's departure set the stage for my leaving. I worked hard not to say "desert" as I once said I would never, ever, desert....no matter what. It was simply time for me to get back to my life, which meant it was time to leave the army.

That night, even with extra guards on the perimeter, I quietly, and gingerly, limped to the stables and lead the Captain's horse, wearing my saddle, from the stall. We crossed the grass and entered a small stream that flowed to the southeast. That black horse and I walked through the darkness and the water until almost daybreak. Then we climbed the bank, I carefully mounted the horse and slowly placed my bruised butt in my saddle. We headed toward the Missouri at a brisk pace.

THE PLAN

Since we didn't have any medical staff at the fort, it would be quite a while before anybody went up to discover that I was no longer in the Post Hospital.   It would take some additional time to find that I wasn't in my bunk or in the kitchen...if anybody was looking. Llewelyn's departure was timely. It was hard to know how long they would pursue him before they either caught him or gave up the chase. Either way, it would be some time before they returned to the Fort and learned of my leaving.

I had forgotten how much ground you can cover on a good horse. We were eating up large amounts of Prairie and the only people we encountered was a freighter going to a trading post in Montana and a family looking for a place to take root along the Missouri. To me, neither of those seemed like a good idea given the situation with the Indians but I had other things on my mind so invested little time and emotion in trying to get them to reconsider.

I intentionally left behind everything

that indicated I was in the Cavalry, with the exception of the horse. Animals like him were few and far between out here and he would draw a lot of attention upon arrival in a settlement. I had also trained the men to take good care of the tack. Too good. Shining leather tack only exists in the Cavalry.

We stopped along a stream to get both of us some water and while I was trying to get my legs and back to cooperate with each other, I decided to give my hat a more civilian look. In the end I took out my frustrations with the military by simply beating the tar out of my hat with a big rock...brim and crown now looked nothing like Cavalry issue. A good scrubbing with some of The Black's recently deposited meadow muffins left me with the look I was wanting...well-used settler.

As I put my foot in the stirrup and tried to get up the courage to boost my butt in the saddle I saw it. No, not it. Them. My stripes. All up and down my leg. Damn. Dead giveaway that I was, or am, in the military. Got to do something about that. The sooner the better.

We skirted the banks of the Missouri for several miles and then came upon a spot where several horses and a couple dozen head of cattle had crossed. This time of year the water is down but it is damned easy to drop into a hole on the Missouri. We picked our way across slowly and made the other bank just as I heard a gunshot. Looking over my shoulder I saw six braves, one with an old powder rifle. They had just wasted gunpowder and a ball. I was too far away.

Their little paint ponies would not make a safe crossing in this part of the river. My 15-hand-tall, well-conditioned, well-trained animal had to work hard to keep up with the current with me mounted on a solid saddle. They knew better than to attempt the crossing on a bare-back. I thought them to be Ottawa which would mean that they were well out of their normal range. We charged up the bank to let the Indians know that if they chose to try it we would be in Saint Joseph before they dried out.

We took to some high ground to see what there was to see. Smoke was coming from four different places to the south and east of our location. This time of day, they wouldn't be campfires. That would leave cabins...people trying to settle into a new place and a future.

I chose the one closest to the river and furthest away. We approached warily as I didn't need anybody anticipating my arrival and welcoming me with a carbine. Behind some Cottonwoods and low-lying willows we tied up and I parted the underbrush to take a closer look at the settlers. There was a small sod building with another built into a hillside, which appeared to be the home. There was a laundry tub in front of the small building and six pieces of clothing were draped across the top rail of a makeshift corral barely capable of keeping a cow and two horses at home. From my viewpoint, it appeared there was a pair of cotton britches that were about my size. I couldn't bring myself to steal the pants... but I would approve of trading them.

I crept as close as I could get in the willows and then stripped off my britches. My red shirt was going to increase my visibility, so I stripped it off and hung it on the backside of one of the Cottonwoods. Now naked, with the exception of my socks and boots, I got low to the ground and made my way to the corral. Don't scare the stock, Graham. GRAHAM? Good God.

I dropped my military issue pants in the tub, grabbed the civilian gear, crouched and ran, as much as possible, until I made the willows. I dressed quickly and was happy to find the pants fit perfectly. I was back in my skivvy shirt and headed back to the saddle.

I thought, "*Wouldn't you just know it.*"

There stood a young boy petting my horse. Just standing there, stroking my horse's mane...and that horse was just about asleep standing up...truly enjoying the attention.

"Ahem," I said and then said again, even louder.

"AWW CRIPES. You scared me, Mister."

"Sorry. I didn't know anyone was here."

"Me, my mother, my father and my little sister."

"No, I mean here," I said, pointing at the ground, "right here....by my horse."

"He's a big horse...and pretty."

"You better say handsome, or you might hurt his feelings."

"Ok. Handsome."

"Well, we need to be on our way."

"What're you doing here?"

"I, uh, had to...uh, you know...uh, squat and take care of some personal needs."

"You do that over by my house?"

"No, over by the trees."

"My father's got a pair of pants like those. They got his letters on them, like our brand. See, T.R...Theodore Rains."

"Well, in my case it stands for, uh...Texas Rangers."

"You a Texas Ranger."

"I can't tell you...but you can't tell anyone I was here because I'm after a fellow."

"What did he do?"

"I can't tell you."

"Where you going?"

"To Fort Atkinson, Nebraska Territory".

"Long ways from what I hear."

"Yep...and I need to get going."

"Thanks for letting me be friends with your horse."

As I was boosting myself into the saddle I heard a distant voice calling for Jeremiah.

"I have to go," he said.

"See you, ...don't tell anybody I was here, Texas Ranger promise?"

"Texas Ranger promise."

I reined in The Black and headed south down the riverbank. As I was just about out of earshot, I heard Jeremiah yell..."Hey, Ranger. Isn't Fort Atkinson over that way?"

CIVIL WAR

Something kept telling me that I needed to get back to Hahn's in Abilene to recover my saddle bags, Henry rifle and the scabbard. The good thing about being to hell-and-gone out there in Fort Atkinson was that there was no place to spend your money and I was carrying quite a fund in my bags. To the best of my recollection, I was almost certain there was silver in those cached saddle bags too.

I turned The Black straight south. Once I get down to St. Joes, I'll choose a direction...for right now I just wanted to put some more distance between me and the Fort. For the next couple of hours the only problem I ran into was fences. On the east side of the Missouri, it seems like everybody built a fence...didn't seem like it was to keep something in, just keeping something out. I spotted a pretty good trail and from where I was sitting, it looked like it was long and straight. I gave The Black the reins and we settled into a loping gait that was smooth and smart, as we used to say in the cavalry.

My mind took me to my memories, my

memories took me to southeast Texas. With no drives to work in the near future and little in terms of capital, I found myself looking for an easy way to make some money. A few months before that I had wandered clear down to Galveston and was taken with the life of a sailor. For the two hours I was out on a sailing ship, I went from excitement, to boredom, to getting rid of my breakfast. Back on solid ground I reminded myself that I was a drover, not a sailor.

Now, here I was heading into Beaumont with the intent of picking my way along the border and coast until I got to somewhere around New Orleans. I figured the Civil War was winding down, from what I heard and read in St. Joes and I could probably find a way to earn some cash.

That was when I was approached by two men in clean, crisp Union uniforms.

"Young man," said the tall one with a smug expression, "May I ask if you are seeking employment?"

"As a matter of fact, I am."

"Would you be interested in serving in the Union effort on behalf of our great country? Pay is $10 per month, and we provide food and lodging."

"Such that it is," said the shorter, very stern fellow.

"I don't have much experience being a soldier," I warned, wondering if I really wanted to be in an outfit that would take me.

The tall guy said, "we'll provide the training you need for what is going on in the war at this time."

The more honest, shorter one continued, "just follow orders, shoot without getting shot and fill in a hole in the company roster. This war is just about over but we need to demonstrate continuing enlistment and strength."

Two hours later while I was waiting for my first orders, Jake Stockman hove into view. Jake was massive. When he rode over the hill, he wasn't ON the horizon, he WAS the horizon. He had the biggest, ugliest horse I had ever seen, aside from those horses that pull the freight wagons in St. Louis...but those were damned good-looking horses, Jake's was just sinfully homely. We all got in line, and I ended up behind Jake, which was to say I couldn't see a thing in front of me but Jake. I went whatever direction he did, and we ended up in line to demonstrate our marksmanship.

Jake had hands that totaled somewhere around two acres. Big, big hands. When he got to his station to shoot the carbine, he couldn't get his index finger between the trigger and the trigger guard without tripping the trigger. Same was true with the Colt revolver.

Just when I was sure he wouldn't be accepted he blurted out, "Why don't you just let me use my own guns?" With that question he was credited with completing his marksmanship trial and he was now a Union Soldier.

My trial went as it should. All of that time at the Fort allowed me to become very proficient with firearms and I immediately fell in behind Jake to get our gear. Full uniforms were in short supply. Some of our other "recruits" were refusing to accept even the coats. Then a burly sergeant stepped out of a tent and bellowed, "Let me explain why it is important for you to wear this coat. When you are out there in these woods in a day or so, if you are wearing this blue coat, only half of the soldiers in the woods with you want to kill you. If you aren't wearing a coat of either color, then ALL of them want to kill you. Do you understand what I am saying?"

Blue coats were, all of the sudden, in great demand with our group of about 20 new soldiers.

Two days later, Jake and I, along with the rest of our new company, were crouched behind two long berms of Louisiana mud, trying to stay out of the rifle sights that came with those blue coats out there.

"Jake, you don't fit behind this bulwark, you're a pretty good target, you know?"

Jake said, with his significant drawl, "In all my 29 years I only been shot once...been shot AT lots of times but only wounded once...and that was me doing the shooting."

"How did that come to be?"

"I had the trigger guard on my revolvers removed so's I could use it with my big ol' fingers"

"Not sure that's a good idea."

"No choice, either do that or learn to shoot with my little finger and that puts the other three in the way of powder burns," he explained. "Anyway, one day I was excited about knocking a coon out of a tree from about a quarter mile away and I forgot to be careful when putting the Colt back in my holster. Trigger caught the edge, gun went off, slug went through the bottom of the holster, into my britches, traveled down my leg, just missed my ankle and blew the whole heel off'n my boot."

"Should have been wearing a different boot or heel."

"What?"

"Never mind."

"Anyway, traced the bullet the entire length of my leg but it didn't get under my skin, so no harm done."

Turns out Jake was an Arkansas boy that lived almost smack dab on top of a line that would label him for Civil War purposes. He had relatives all over that neck of the mountains, some ended up Gray, some Blue.

For the next four months we marched, hiked, walked, stumbled and grumbled through not very well-organized campaigns. Some involved shooting. Most involved just being seen. The big battles were being fought in the north, east and south. We were just here to make sure nothing went wrong in the west.

One day we were hiding in some rocks on a hillside, waiting for what we were told would be a few wagons with supplies for the Confederacy. I looked over at Jake and said, "does it make sense to continue to kill these men when this thing is about done?"

He looked me straight in the eye and said, "I been thinking the same thing."

"How about we agree to just wound them...you know, an arm or leg".

"Yes. Which one should it be?"

"I'm thinking left arm. Just a little more than a flesh wound so they'll be done with the fighting and then it will be over."

"I agree, Private Graham, this is a good plan."

For the next four weeks, we only shot for the body on two occasions.

The first, we had no choice. About sunset one evening, six of us were returning to the camp when we came out of a thicket, only to be face-to-face with four blue jackets. We had numbers so we figured they would surrender.

"Put your weapons down and surrender. There is no need for more killing," yelled our Corporal.

The Rebs talked quietly for a minute and then each raised one hand, indicating they were going to drop their rifles and side arms.

Jake whispered "Don't believe them. It's an old mountain trick."

He had no sooner said that when they dropped to a knee and brought their rifles up to fire. The tactic was a bad decision because we hadn't lowered our rifles. All four fell to the ground. Three dead, one wounded.

The gunfire brought more soldiers, and we withdrew back into the thicket to make our way to the camp.

The Corporal said Jake's warning probably saved us.

Jake's response was "actin' like you're

giving up is something you learn early in my mountains. Buys time and fools your enemy."

Three days later eight of us were on patrol along a creek that had several large rocks in the bottom. We found ourselves between a steep bank and seven Rebel rifles. When they stepped out from behind the boulders we froze. Now the boot was on the other foot.

Jake whispered, "Make 'em think we're surrendering."

The six of us that were together three days earlier understood the plan. The other two would have to create their own.

We raised our right hand and started to lay the rifles down.

In the volley that followed three from each side died. One wounded on our side and two on theirs. The rest of us just standing there wondering what to do next.

If the event that was just about to take place had not happened, we would have probably all turned and walked away but that was not to be. One of the Rebels that was wounded was lying against a rock, bleeding from a wound in his stomach. Jake and I made our way over to see if there was anything we could do. From about ten feet away the Reb cried out "Jacob!"

Jake stood upright, stared and then

called back "Moses!" as he ran toward the injured man.

Jake bent over to help and, as he did so, a shot rang out from the right. The other injured rebel had shot at Jake from almost point-blank range.

Jake went to the ground and my bayonet ended a coward's life...that wasn't battle, that was a killing. I went to Jake's side, but it was obvious that he was mortally wounded. Blood gushed from the neck wound and I put my hand over it in a futile attempt to keep him alive.

"Moses was my cousin. My best friend. Now we die together," and with that, he was gone.

That night, during a changing of the perimeter guards, I hung my blue coat on a tree branch near my tent...and left the Union Army. Earlier, when we got back to camp, we buried our dead and listened to the courier that had arrived while we were gone. The Civil War was over.

Two months later, in a saloon on the outskirts of Houston, a fellow that had most certainly not been involved in the Civil War made the statement that anybody that signed on only for the money was nothing more than a goddamned mercenary. I guess he figured nobody in there that night would understand the meaning of the word. Moments later, as I walked out through the swinging doors rubbing the pain out of my knuckles on my right hand, I was certain the fellow laying on the floor in there would have to forego solid food for a couple of days.

An unconscious flexing of my right hand brought me back to the Missouri River. I had just come to the top of a hill and was looking down on the railyards in the city of Atchison, Kansas Territory. I gave The Black a solid pat on the mane to thank him for taking care of me while I was away somewhere else.

MR. RAINS OF ATCHISON

From the hilltop I could see where the ferry crossed the Missouri and we set about getting down there before it got much darker than it already was. I stopped short of the landing and dug into my saddlebags. I was now back to where I would have to use money and didn't see any sense in letting anybody know I had coin in my bags. Dropping it in the pockets of Mr. Rains former britches I felt it slide right down my leg and bounce down into my boots.

"Wouldn't you know it? I traded for a pair of pants that has a hole in the pocket."

I poked at the other side pocket, and it seemed to work so I dumped my boot and deposited the jingle in it.

The ferry was just sliding into the landing and one other horse and rider were waiting. I walked The Black onto the Ferry and tied him to a hitch ring. The other passenger was really studying The Black, even to the point of walking around him as we departed the landing.

"Something I might do for you?" I asked with a slight edge to my voice.

"Your horse wouldn't happen to be for sale, would he?" asked the man with a carefully fitted straw hat.

"At this point in my life, everything I have is for sale. You buying?"

"No, not me, but I have a livestock business and I have a client that is interested in a 15-16 hand horse that's in good physical condition. Yours is, indeed, a handsome specimen."

I felt my left pocket getting heavier from all of the currency I was going to be dropping in there in the near future, "Look, I've been riding for the last couple of days and I'm way past tired. If you would be so kind as to direct me to the finest livery in town, I'll get The Black to rest and then I'll do the same. If your client wants to see the horse, we will be here until 11 tomorrow at the stable and we can talk then."

"Patzen's is the best. They take care of most of the more successful people's horses here in Atchison. When you get off the Ferry go a block, turn right and Patzen's is on the next corner. I expect we will be seeing you at 11 o'clock tomorrow morning."

With that, we were arriving at the opposite shore and The Black and I headed for Patzen's Stables.

After days of saddles and soil, a hotel

room, regardless of the condition of the mattress is one of the great pleasures of life. When I checked in the clerk looked me up and down and then said, with a certain sense of urgency, "Sir, I'm sure you intend to purchase a bath prior to taking advantage of our superior furnishings here at the Radcliffe. I can ask that one be drawn up for you immediately. With your permission we will also launder your clothes overnight and they will be fresh for you when you want them delivered to your room."

Since I was feeling rich and dusty, all of that made sense.

"How much is all that going to cost me, Edward?" I asked, surveying his name badge on his chest.

"Two dollars for the room and a dollar for the bath and laundry," Edward said, with a smile.

No decision to be made there. I tossed my gear in the room, did a quick test of the condition of the mattress, gave it a nod of approval and went straight to the bath chambers. A tub was, indeed, drawn with a wisp of steam wiggling through the night air. The middle-aged lady that reached through the door to take my clothes to the laundry room took a sneak peek through the opening and said "Now if you need anything else this evening you make sure you let me know. Name's Matilda and I'm at the end of the hall in the Laundry Room."

I mulled the content and true intent of the message for a moment, climbed into the tub and stayed there until the water was no longer warmer than my body. After a final rinse, I wrapped a towel around my ivory white frame and headed for my room. Two steps out of the bath chambers Matilda appeared out of the Laundry Room and asked how the bath was.

"Just about as fine an experience as I can imagine, Matilda. Absolutely a joy. My thanks for your assistance."

Just after daybreak I was awakened by a noise at my door. Matilda was leaving my room to get my clothing and shortly thereafter I went in search of a good breakfast, which, in a railroad town, is never a problem.

I got back up to Patzen's a little early to spruce up The Black. From the door I could tell that he, too, had benefitted from a bath. I asked the hand that was feeding the horses if he did it and, if so, why.

"Mr. Meyer asked that I bathe the horse in advance of the 11:00 showing. He paid me and gave me a right handsome tip too." said the boy of 13 or 14.

"This guy, Meyer, is pretty slick. Knows his stuff. Guess I better figure out how high I can go on this horse before they get here."

I had just decided that such a fine horse should be worth about fifty dollars when I heard "ahem" behind me. Meyer had arrived. He wanted to talk pricing and commissions and history and things I didn't want to talk about.

"Mr. Meyer, I'll tell you what. If we can reach agreement on my $50 price, then you can reach your agreements with the buyer. As far as history, I got this horse when I left the military. When the war was over, they gave me the horse and my papers at the same time. Plenty long ago now. That do it for you?"

Just as Meyer was going to renegotiate the price or take exception with something I said, a big ol' boy in a banker's suit came striding into the stable.

"Good Morning, Abraham," said Mr. Meyer.

"Good Morning, Albert, beautiful day."

With that the stable hand presented The Black to Abraham and Albert. I swear that at one point the horse turned his head to look at me with a "what the hell is this all about, anyway?".

Abraham walked slowly around the

horse, checking the hooves, teeth, eyes and hips.

"Where did this horse come from?" asked Abraham. My mostly true story that I presented before was delivered again with certain proper embellishments.

"This tack looks to be US Cavalry issue. How did you come to have it?"

"You have a good eye, Sir. May I ask your name?"

"You already have Abraham. Last name is Stockman".

"Of the Arkansas Stockman?"

He stopped looking at the horse and his eyes burned into mine.

"How do you know of my family?"

"Fought with one and against one. Both died, I'm sorry to say."

"Union?"

"Yes, Sir."

"Jacob?"

"Yes, but we knew him as Jake. 'Bout the best man I ever met. Loved him like a brother. Died like the hero he was."

"We lost three on the Blue side."

"Moses?"

"We always wondered what happened to him. There was never any communication."

As we stood there in the dusty stable I

shared the story about their last minutes of life.

The silence was deafening when I finished. Abraham turned and walked away without saying a word. He went to the door of the stable, stared out at nothing in particular, turned and came back into the stable, all the time drying his eyes.

"I can't begin to tell you how much your story means to me and will mean to our family. This brings the whole unfortunate war to an end for us," he said.

He took another deep breath and then proceeded to press for more information about The Black.

"This horse wasn't with you in Louisiana, it's too young. Where did you get the horse and the tack?"

"Horse came with my departure from the Cavalry at Fort Atkinson. If they hadn't given it to me it surely would have died in last winter's killing weather."

"Yes. Terrible it was. We kept listening for news to come down."

"The tack is a gift to help me remember my father. My family was stationed at Fort Scott, Kansas Territory. My father was an officer and was killed in Mexico. At 16 I departed the Fort. The Fort Commandant presented me with the tack I used on my horse there."

"Tragic story. Beautiful and moving, but tragic," said Abraham, quietly.

All of the sudden the panic of remembering who I was, or wasn't, stormed into my mind.

"I'm afraid I don't know who you are," Abraham said, almost apologetically.

"Theodore Rains. I had a small farm up the Missouri but have decided to head for Colorado to see if I can strike it rich in the gold fields."

"I noticed the monogram on your britches and wondered what it stood for."

"Same as my brand. Not a very successful venture, however."

"Yes, tough business," intoned Mr. Meyer, who had wisely stayed quiet in the background.

"So, Mr. Rains. How much do you want for this beautiful horse?"

"I was thinking $50."

"Oh, so he comes with a surrey or some other wagon? He must, at that price."

"Hard to give up so much history and so many miles," I offered.

"Yes, I'm sure it is. Here is my offer. I'll give you 40 but I want you to keep the tack. It's family."

"Fact is that I don't intend to replace the

horse. In the Rockies, horses are almost unusable. I need the money more than anything else."

Then the smart side of my brain slapped me upside the ear... *"that's evidence!"*.

Before Abraham could say anything else I blurted out..."no, you're right. I need the bridle. Forty dollars it is."

He handed over the money, I handed over the horse to Mr. Meyer and he slipped a rope halter on The Black. Abraham handed over the bridle and I gathered up my gear and turned to head down the street to the railroad station. No sense in dragging out the good-byes. We had all burned up about as much emotion as we could afford to.

"One ticket to Abilene, please. Kansas, not Texas."

RETURN TO HAHN'S

This being a paying passenger and sitting in an upholstered seat in the railcar is a much different experience that jumping a ride in a cattle car. Those long-horned Longhorns make it very uncomfortable. I have never heard of anybody being intentionally gored by one of those weapons sticking out of their head but there are many instances where an accidental impaling created a great deal of stress and a little blood. I had learned from experience that you get to the front corner of the car for travel in the summer and in the middle of the back wall for the winter. Moving air in the summer, body heat in the winter. But this, riding as a passenger, was another experience all together. Watching the country go by made me think this was the way to travel. Wherever I decide to go in the future would definitely include being a passenger.

The six-hour ride, much of which was spent stopped for additional wood and water, was just starting to make my butt tired so I was glad to see the outskirts of Abilene come into view.

I still had my requisitioned bridle that I needed to address. It was just starting to get dark as I turned the corner and could see Hahn's Stable. His horse and buggy weren't in front so I figured they were closed, and this might be a good time to go in and tunnel to my saddle bags and scabbard.

Stepping up to the entrance, I yelled my finest "Halllloooo". No response. I walked on in and asked if anybody was there. Nothing. I dropped my gear in an empty stall and climbed the ladder up into the hayloft. It was dark as midnight in there, but I knew all I had to do was stay on the floor, crawl along until I hit the wall and go left until I reached the corner.

About four feet into the hay pile I touched something hairy and warm, which none of my property would be. I almost wished it was a person, but the noise told me it wasn't. I grabbed it with both hands and tossed it across the floor. As it righted itself and scurried away, I saw enough of it to know it was a possum. Ugly little beasts. Hoped that was the only one.

From what I could tell, about half of the hay was gone but there was enough that nobody would have stumbled onto the scabbard and bags while forking hay from the loft to downstairs.

I went back on the floor and burrowed with a little more attention being paid now. I knew I had to be almost the end of the loft when I felt leather....and I was glad that it wasn't moving.

Sure enough, it was my scabbard. I stood up, pushed the hay out of my way and confirmed the Sharps Repeating Rifle was still in there. They were known as Beecher's Bible in this part of the territory. I reverently laid it on the floor and went back into the mountain of forage.

Finally, I felt more leather. Flaps. Had to be my saddlebags. When I stood up this time there was light. A kerosene lantern had been lit and there was somebody holding it with their left hand... a Colt in the right.

"Howdy," I said, trying to speak without evidence of surprise or uncertainty.

"Who are you and what in the world are you doing up here?"

"My name is...uh...Theodore Rains and I'm a little short on cash so I was hoping to sleep up here tonight."

"That your gear downstairs in the stall?"

"Yep. Couldn't figure out how to carry all of this stuff up here at the same time and still survive the ladder."

"Probably a good decision."

"Can I ask if you are the proprietor?"

"Not yet. Going to buy it. The owner is not well and doesn't want to give it up until he dies."

"You going to have me arrested for...well, I guess...trespassing?"

"Don't think so. This is kind of an interesting time here in Abilene. The former Marshal was a good man and very sensible. This new one's kind of different. Hard to tell how he is going to respond to anything."

"Last time I was in town there was a Texas Ranger here. He still here? He could give you a good word on me."

"Rangers don't come up here much anymore unless they are after someone that committed a serious crime in Texas and they're on the run."

"Interesting...and disappointing at the same time. So, who is the Marshal now?"

"None other than William Hickok. Wild Bill, hisself."

"Working as a lawman?"

"Yep."

"Don't need to bother him, no, I don't. If you're all right, I'll just gather my stuff and leave."

"I guess so. I don't want any of his time or attention either. You seem like a decent sort. Why don't you just bunk in up here, I'll forget I found you."

"I surely do appreciate it."

"Be quiet and don't burn the place down."

"I will...and I won't."

I lay there for about a half hour before I gathered up my gear, clambered down the ladder and headed toward the door with two saddlebags, a scabbard, rifle and a bridle.

At the door I set the pile of gear on the floor, went over to a wall peg and removed five or six bridles that had been hanging there for quite some time, judging by the dirt stacked on them. I placed my Cavalry bridle on the peg, loaded the others back on top of it and walked out of that stable without the physical or emotional burden that goes along with being in possession of cavalry gear.

I headed for the nearest hotel so as to get a good night's sleep.

DEALING WITH THE LAW

I had heard from several men over the last couple of years that the marshal in Abilene was a good man. He brought order to this town...and did it without having to use his guns.

Tom Smith was from back East somewhere and chose to use his fists to make sure his position was understood. As his pugilistic reputation spread, troublemakers came to understand that you couldn't goad him into a gunfight because he would just walk right up to you and break your jaw. In most cases, most men are only brave when they have a "Peacemaker" in their hand. If it comes down to knowing you will have to protect yourself from a raging bull of a man with only your fists, you choose not to pick the fight in the first place.

I had come to the opinion that I should have come back to Abilene earlier before Marshal Smith left his position to join the Texas Rangers.

Wild Bill Hickok is a different thing. His reputation was based on a lightning-fast draw and an even faster temper...neither of which I had any desire to witness, even as an observer. He had honestly earned his moniker.

Morning arrived with a blazing hot sun. Kansas Territory comes with the fires of hell in the summers. I headed down to the table to take on some breakfast before I had a large sip of Rye. Then I would make up my mind what I would do. For the first time, possibly in my entire life, I figured I had several options available to me. I wasn't carrying any extra baggage, unless you want to consider not having an identity. I had coin in my bags, wrapped tight so's not to make any noise when I set the bags down. Got my Sharps and scabbard. If I'm not leaving on a train, I'll need a horse and a saddle. Otherwise, buy a ticket and watch the territory go by my railroad car windows. On my second plate full of pig and potatoes I started thinking about Lubbock.

It wasn't lost on me that returning to Texas would fall somewhere in the "really bad idea" bucket. No doubt the law, including the Texas Rangers, were looking for me and if that deputy went on to die, there is probably a price on my head. I reminded myself that they aren't looking for me, they were on the lookout for some not-very-clever young man named Andy

Graham. I have to admit that I look a little bit like Andy Graham but if I were to get a barber shop shave and haircut, I would probably be so handsome that no one could confuse me for that rash little man suffering from poor judgement.

After all, the only person that could identify me for certain was one pretty little lady...the very one that got me in all this trouble to begin with.

"That's not true or fair. All she did was look pretty walking down the boardwalk".

If I could find her again, maybe she would forgive me for my ways. She knows that I didn't pull the trigger on that deputy because I had my arms around her. Protecting her from the melee, that's what I was doing......being her guardian, temporarily.

I walked into the Atchison, Topeka and Santa Fe office at the depot and asked about a ticket to Lubbock.

"Can't sell it to you," replied the clerk as he slowly raised his head to respond.

"Why?"

"Railroad don't go there...yet."

"How close can I get?"

"Abilene."

"Kansas or Texas?"

"Texas."

"OK. How much is that?"

"Eight Dollars. Remember now, you're going to have to change trains two times to get to Abilene. Likely take you four days."

"I got time," I said, all the time wondering if I really wanted to spend four days sitting in a railroad car.

"You will have to buy a ticket each time you get to the next railroad."

"So that $8 isn't the total cost then I take it."

"Nope. Probably be in the range of twenty, all things considered.

Then I realized I would have to buy a horse in Abilene to get to Lubbock.

I headed over to Hahn's to see what he had for stock.

My shadow had barely darkened the floor of the stable when I heard a familiar voice welcoming me.

"Mr. Rains. I wondered what had become of you."

"Thanks to your hospitality I got a couple hours of rest and then found my way to a poker game. Outcome was never in doubt. Now, what can we work out so I can be on my way with four hooves under me?"

We had just arrived at the corral behind the stable when two men cornered the building, one of them wearing a badge.

"Thornburg! Doc asked me to come over. He said to tell you Old Man Hahn died last night," said the man wearing the badge.

"I was afraid the end was near, Marshal Hickok, as he didn't recognize me the last time I visited with him."

"There has been some discussion about whether or not to bring charges against the men that beat him so badly. Doc thinks the injuries hastened his demise. I had heard that a Texas Ranger tracked two of them down and brought them back here for burial. Undertaker said he put them in one hole up at on Pauper's Hill. So, from all of that, it appears that one of the gang got away. I'm not thinking it is a good use of law time to go looking for the third after all this time."

I really wanted to give Hickok the whole story but thought better of it. My rapt attention to the story must have caught Hickok's eye.

"Now, who might you be?" asked the Marshal, eyeballing me and eventually fixing his gaze on my face.

I guessed I would be making Wild Bill's acquaintance.

"Theodore Rains, Marshal."

"And where would Mr. Rains hale from?"

"Most recently a settler on the east side of the Missouri but now headed to Lubbock and return to my life as a drover."

Thornburg interrupted, "I thought you were heading to Colorado and the gold fields."

"Got to thinking about it and decided being a drover creates regular pay. Finding gold can't be as easy as people make it sound or it wouldn't be worth as much money as it is."

Hickok had been studying my face.

"If I were to go over to my office and look through my wanted posters, would I find you in the stack?"

"Hate to disappoint you, Marshal. Can't even find a lady that wants me, so certainly not the law."

"Umm-Hmmm. Care to walk over to the office with me?" His question didn't come across as an invitation but rather an order.

"It would be a pleasure, Marshal."

"Umm-Hmmm.

"Mr. Thornburg, how much is that Roan Gelding?"

"Twelve dollars."

"Will a total of $15 get me a good saddle too?"

"Yes, Sir!"

"I'll be back to get him and settle up as soon as I finish with Marshal Hickok."

"I close at six, you remember."

"Yes, Mr. Thornburg, I remember."

As we walked right down the middle of the street, horses, wagons and people alike all seemed to move to the side for the Marshal. If was clear that his "Wild Bill" reputation was both earned and understood.

"Sit down right there," he ordered as motioned to the cot in a cell while he grabbed a pile of leaflets from the desk.

"Now, what was your name again?"

I guess I delayed a little too long in making sure I was using the right name.

"What's the problem? Forget who you are?"

"No Sir. I was just wondering if you wanted my middle name too."

"Nope."

"Theodore Rains. Closest town to my ranch was Atchison."

"I see your brand on your britches."

"Yes Sir."

"'Bout all I got left from that venture."

"Tough business. Especially with the winter we had last. Lost a lot of stock and people in that one."

"That is the truth."

"Well, I don't see anybody in here that looks enough like you to look any further. Say, if you're from that neck of the woods, maybe you saw this deserter."

DESERTER!

My heart virtually stopped beating.

Hickok held up the wanted poster for one Timothy Llewelyn, a deserter from Fort Atkinson, Nebraska Territory.

"No Sir. Wish I could help you," was about as useless a comment as I could make but it seemed to do as intended. It got me out of there and headed for Hahn's.

"Good Lord, if that's the best drawing they are doing for those posters, I'm in good shape.   That didn't look anything like Llewelyn."

Less than an hour later I had a pretty comfortable saddle on the back of a pretty good looking 15 hand gelding and I was southbound along the Chisolm Trail.

OLD FRIENDS

It had been said for years that Texas cattlemen only bred the skeletons of the Longhorn. It was their trip through the prairies of Kansas Territory that put the meat on them. Drovers knew that to be true. The Chisholm, and most of the other trails that went through the Bluestem Grassland Prairies, were known to provide some of the best forage for the herds going north.

Once you got deep into Kansas Territory and arrived at the railroads that would ship the stock to the eastern markets you had a finished animal...Going further north wasn't as good a situation. It wasn't only because there was less grass, but the distance and the weather would often take its toll too.

Over the years the trails had become wider and wider to provide the grazing the herds needed. For that reason it was damned easy to ride south along the Chisholm and I was making great time, except for the fact that I kept running into fellows that I had known over the years past.

When the herd is moving the drovers are too. When I would hear a familiar whoop or call or hear someone call my name I would be required to fall in beside the drover and ride back north as we visited. That meant that I often would be covering the same ground a second time to make up the dirt I tracked while catching up on a man's life.

One such occasion was mid-afternoon just a few hours north of the little watering hole that had a couple of buildings built around it. Folks thereabouts were coming to call the place Wichita, which I always figured was the white man's way of spelling the name of the Oachita, a tribe somehow related to the Cherokees but ranging up north a bit further. I was just easing my way south, on the western edge of a large herd when I came upon one of the outriders going the north. As he came closer I couldn't help but notice the scars across his face and forehead.

"Bear. Had to be. Big deep, ragged scars. That has to be the story."

"As we met, the rider looked me straight in the eyes. His stare was making me a little uneasy. I could tell he was studying me, and he was certainly startled when I gave him my half-assed salute as a friendly gesture. He almost spun his head off looking backward at me as he went north, me south. Less than a quarter mile later, hoof beats told me somebody was closing fast...and then the yell that, I swear, stopped my heart.

"DRISCOLL! Driscoll, hold up!"

"Driscoll? Who would know me as Driscoll? Worse yet, how easy was it to recognize me?"

I reined in my horse and waited for the rider to come up beside me.

"Driscoll. Am I right? Is that you?"

"Who wants to know?" I asked, hoping to get a name that would help me to feel safe again.

"It's me. Llewelyn. The deserter."

It was startling to me that he said "deserter" with no indication of shame or remorse. I stared intently at his face, wanting desperately to recognize Llewellyn so as to confirm his identity.

"Llewelyn. You're still with us. I'm glad to see that."

I couldn't help but stare, again, at the two scars that ran in a ragged fashion across his forehead and right cheek. He caught my study, and with a little smile chuckled, saying "that's a result of my discharge".

We sat there on our horses while I listened to his story. For seven days after he left the fort he had covered considerable ground and, he felt, he was staying ahead of the soldiers pursuing him.

Near to a little town of Lecompton in Kansas Territory he found himself in the midst of a running battle between the remnants of two armies, one of abolitionists and another willing to battle to keep slaves.

"I didn't have a dog in that hunt but that didn't make any difference. They just figured I was one of them or the other and, as a result, I ended up taking a tree branch across the forehead," he said as he rubbed his fingertips across his scar.

"It took a while to find somebody willing to work on my wound because I was a stranger and nobody knew my leanings. Finally found a dentist that would sew me back together."

"Two days later some soldiers from Fort Leavenworth arrived and started asking questions about the stranger that had recently arrived in the area."

"Early the next morning, four men arrived at my campsite just as I mounted my horse. They told me they knew I was Llewelyn and that I was going to be arrested for desertion."

"I repeated a number of times that I was not Llewelyn but it was hard to profess such a thing when I was sitting on one of the fort's saddles on one of the fort's horses," he chuckled again, as he recalled the absurdity of the situation.

"Just as I leaned back and swung my leg over for a dismount, I felt the blade run down my cheek. It was obvious that one of them had tried to cut my throat but missed when I moved. I fell to the ground, rolled under my horse and punched the poor animal in the gut. He started bucking, snorting and creating all sorts of chaos. Meanwhile I crawled through flying hooves and ran into the forest where they couldn't come on horseback. By the time they got their horses settled down, dismounted and tied up, I had a good lead."

"I figured that after so many days on horseback they wouldn't have their walking legs under them, let alone their runnin' ones. The other thing I knew was that there were about 30 of those pro-slavery guys that were camped a little less than half a mile away. They were on edge and wouldn't take kindly to a bunch of US Cavalry men running through their outfit."

"So I ran through their camp like a jackrabbit, yelling that the army was coming for us. Most every one of those men were standing upright and ready when the soldiers came charging into the clearing and saw some 30 muzzles pointed at them. I wish I'd a had time to stop and watch," he said, chuckling again.

Just as he finished another outrider came wheeling toward us, screaming "Ewing, do you want to come in for your final pay or you going to catch up with the herd and do your job?"

"Ewing.   That's fitting. A final tribute. Good for you, Llewelyn."

"Good to see you again, hope it's not the last time we stand on the same piece of ground," he yelled as he reined his horse over hard and raced to catch up with the herd and his life as Ewing.

I sat there for a minute, reflecting on the conversation. *"I didn't have to admit that I left the military. I'm pleased I didn't have to say it. I'm not sure I know why, I just didn't want to have to say it."*

WICHITA

The trail going north along this route became known as the Chisholm because old Jesse Chisholm had been plying this dirt for years with this teams and wagons. He was a trader and a teamster. Half Irish and Half Cherokee, he was fluent in two languages and 9 or 10 dialects of the tribes from throughout the middle of the country.

Over the years he had trapped, traded and explored just about everything and everyplace that was out there between deep south Texas and Abilene...Kansas, way past Texas.

While doing so he had discovered all the best places to camp, all the best water and all the best places to ford the rivers. He also knew that the deep, lush tall grass prairie would grow just about any animal. His understanding of the people and nature of that long stretch through Texas, Indian Territory and Kansas Territory made him very important to the companies that would use "his" trail to move their livestock north.

He was frequently asked to participate

in conversations with Indians when it came time to put a treaty in place. He knew the language, yes, but more importantly, the Indians and white man alike trusted Jesse Chisholm...a man of great integrity.

One of the sites that Chisholm came to enjoy deeply was where the Big Arkansas and Little Arkansas Rivers came together. Settlers started to consider the confluence as a town site and that was where Wichita would come to be. My return to the "town" provided several surprises. Last time I was through there were some tents and a pile of waste wood that was the trading post. Now I saw about three dozen or so real buildings and dirt that had been trampled into something that resembled streets.

Since it was late in the day and every part of my body begged to get out of the saddle and stirrups, I stopped at the post and inquired if there was a hotel in town.

"Last week, I'd a said, nope, but this week the answer is 'yes'," replied a talkative clerk behind a table that should have had four legs but instead had three and a keg.

"Would you be so kind as to direct me to the establishment?"

"That's a big word for Witch-A-Taw", he said, putting a specific emphasis on each syllable. "I'm thinking you could go out the door and look for a sign that says 'Hole-Tell'."

"Many thanks," I said, looking for an opportunity to escape out the door.

I stood there in the dust, looking up and down the street for a sign on the hotel. Nothing. A lad of about 10 came walking by carrying a tin of milk. I asked if he could point me to the hotel.

"Munger's. It's their house. 10th. 10th and Waco," he volunteered.

I stood there considering whether or not I wanted to drink the water here. Seems to make for some interesting people. Makes them have complicated conversations.

"Wichita has street names?"

"Yes, sir. Streets and Avenues. You are on 10th. Waco is two blocks down there."

"Appreciate your capable assistance," I said, using some of my Fort Scott education.

There were only two structures on that side of 10th. One was clearly a blacksmith. The other was a two-story log building that, though small, certainly could be a hotel. As I approached the building, I noticed two slabs of cottonwood painted and nailed to the skeleton of a long dead tree. Waco on one. 10 on the other.

I just stood at the crossroads and laughed, shaking my head. Didn't make any difference which way I looked from there, no other "streets" or signs were to be seen.

I stepped up on the porch and stood directly in front of the door, trying to decide if I should just walk in or if I should knock since it looked like somebody's home. I wondered if there was another entrance carrying a "hotel" sign. I leaned back to see what could be seen as I proceeded to knock on the door but instead of my knuckle rapping on wood I felt a resilient, fabric surface. It took no time at all for my face to flush with blood when I realized I had just tapped upon a young lady's chest. She had opened the door and stepped out as I knocked. We were now intimately acquainted.

"Well, now, aren't you something?" she said, looking into my eyes with a trace of a mischievous smile on her face.

I couldn't get my mouth to move or my lips to form words. My stammering and stuttering was becoming an additional embarrassment...and then she said "You had best figure out a way to get yourself together now, I don't have time to wait while you learn to speak."

....and then she was gone, moving briskly down Waco Street.

I was still working through the injury to my ego when I heard a decidedly mature male voice ask, "Young man, is there something I can help you with?"

"Yes, Sir. I was hoping to bunk at the hotel tonight if there is a room," I said, observing how much easier it was to speak to this very distinguished gentleman than to the lady whose bosom I had bruised a few minutes ago.

"I'm afraid accommodations here in Wichita are somewhat sparse at this time in our existence," he said matter-of-factly, "but we are growing quickly, and many more amenities will be available in the coming months."

"Sir, I, too, believe that will be true."

He studied me for a minute and then cocked his head, "Interesting. Your attire, demeanor and language are inconsistent. Interesting, indeed."

While I was thinking about what, if anything, to say in response to that comment, the young lady I accidentally assaulted returned, walking as if on a mission. She disappeared into the house without acknowledging my existence or making a sound.

"Allow me to introduce myself. I am Darius Munger, the proprietor of the Munger House Hotel. I, my wife and our three daughters reside in the home and offer two beds for travelers. Each is $1 per night. Meals are fifty cents apiece."

"I believe I have met Mrs. Munger as we bumped into each other when I arrived," I said, delicately trying to choose my words wisely.

"You're mistaken. That was my oldest daughter, I would imagine. She is 17 years of age, I believe, and will take responsibility for the hotel as we expand."

"I'm sorry....no, not sorry that she will manage the hotel......sorry for the faulty assumption that she was Mrs. Munger," I stammered. *"Damn. She's still doing it, still making it difficult to be, or even appear to be, coherent."*

"Mr. Munger, do you, by chance, have a bed for me this evening?"

"Yes, I believe we do. Would you be dining with us?"

"It would be an honor."

"Splendid. We can get acquainted over dinner."

He led me into the parlor, through the dining area and into one big room that had two beds in it. That was the extent of the accommodations, "We, our family, live upstairs so we ask that you be mindful of our presence."

"I most certainly will be, sir. Is there a

place in town to get a shave and bath?"

"Go over to 9th Street. It's the barbershop on the corner. O'Hara's. But make sure you get back at seven o'clock. That's dinner. Seven sharp."

"Yes, Sir." I walked out of the Munger House, turned left on Waco, took 20 steps and found myself at O'Hara's. Spartan, it was. One chair for workin', one for waitin', O'Hara himself, a curtain and a sitting tub. That was it but that was all I needed.

"Howdy. O'Hara's the name."

"Graham. Andrew Graham. Friends call me 'Andy' and I consider you to be my friend."

"Andrew Graham! It just tumbled out of my mouth like it was supposed to. I didn't even have to think about it. Andrew Graham."

"Pleased to be your friend, Andy Graham," replied the amiable barber, "What brings you to Wichita?"

"My horse, since there isn't a railroad through here. Headed to Lubbock."

"That's good humor, Andy. A very good response. True too, it is. You know we just decided to incorporate and become a city. There are big plans for this camp. One day, we'll be just as important as Abilene, Atchison and even Kansas City and St. Joes, maybe."

"Good spot in the right place. Got a future, I think."

"Staying long?"

"Overnight. Munger House."

"Before long we'll have the Southern Hotel open and that will be a first-class operation. Right now the Mungers are having to serve almost every civic duty and need. Good people. Very good people."

"I need to be cut and clean by seven. That's dinner according to Mr. Munger."

"Yes, you do, but we have plenty of time to get you all cleaned up. Better be with your best manners. Darius is forthright but Mrs. Munger is a terror if you get on the wrong side of her. You can ask me and I can tell you. The next one to be aware of is Katie. She's the oldest daughter."

"I know she looks innocent and helpless, but she could take down a buffalo with one arm. Watched her backhand a drunken drover outside of Fritz Snitzler's Saloon one night when she was walking home with her sister. He said something he shouldn't have said. She told him so. He started to talk back and a few minutes later it took four of us to carry him over to the veterinarian's office to put some of his teeth back in. Big and strong, body and mind, that's what she is."

"Yes. We have met each other. Solid, certainly solid. Says what's on her mind. Seems she has a need to get things off her chest," I said, enjoying my clever attempt at humor and pleased to have an opportunity to relive the moment.

"Yes. That would be true enough. Say, Andy, would you be inclined to rinse some trail dust out of your mouth before you sit in that tub?"

"I would enjoy, appreciate and worship a Rye Whiskey right now."

O'Hara stepped to the open door and yelled for the young man I had met earlier.

"Daniel, come on in here will you. Daniel, Andy. Daniel, would you run up to Snitzler's and get two Ryes and bring them back here? Hurry now, will you?"

"Daniel helped me find the Munger House when I got into town."

"Daniel talked to you? That is very unusual. Not that he is particularly bashful or backward. Just doesn't talk to most anybody. He's almost fifteen but most would take him for five years less than that. Good boy. Dependable and honest."

"He was very cordial and helpful."

"He must consider you a friend."

Following the shave, the Rye and my bath I made my way back to Munger's just in time to be seated. The Munger's were doing a fine job of raising their children. Each had their tasks for the meal and the meal was followed by some entertaining and far-reaching conversations between the children. Following dinner, Darius and his wife, who had been in the kitchen during the meal, departed for the evening services at the Presbyterian Church. I returned to Fritz Snitzler's Saloon for the last two drinks of Rye that were left in the bottle. One I drank in the saloon and the bottle I took to the parlor at Munger's.

I made myself comfortable in a horsehair-stuffed chair and took my first sip of the last Rye when I sensed her eyes burning through me from the darkness of the dining room.

"Katie? Is that you in there?"

"Yes."

"Well, come on out and visit with me".

"I'd rather be in a buffalo stampede."

"Why on earth?"

"Drinking makes men to terrible things."

"Well, not all drinks and certainly not all men."

"Seems so to me."

"Would you mind telling me why you feel that way?"

"Yes. NO! I mean yes, I would mind

telling you."

"OK. Now you're starting to sound like me when I knocked on your chest earlier today. I'm so very sorry that happened. I didn't know you had opened the door. Again, I'm sorry, please forgive me as I am not a man to touch a woman...I mean, without her telling me I can."

"So, a woman is supposed to say 'yes, you can touch me'?"

"Well, yes, if she wants him to."

"And what if she doesn't....I mean, uh, want him....to touch her, I mean?"

"That's what she needs to say. Today was a terrible mistake. I wasn't watching what I was doing."

"I wasn't offended by your touching me. The look on your face made me laugh. I'll remember that expression on your face forever."

"I'm just pleased that you were not offended by my hands touching you...I mean, you know, uh...there....in that manner."

"I'm not sure I understand why I felt the way I did...and the way I do."

She moved across the floor and was standing next to my chair when she whispered, "Yes. You can touch me."

ADIOS

I was up with the sun, feeling the need to get on the trail. Truth be known, I didn't know how I would handle seeing or talking to Katie. It was four blocks to the stables and I was talking to myself while I made my way. I knew the right thing, the best thing and the gentleman's thing to do was to go to breakfast, which I had already paid for, sit there and act like a boarder that was soon to be on his way.

I visited with the veterinarian that owned the livery stable while I got the roan saddled up. He, too, wanted to talk about all the plans for Wichita. He was concerned about how the Cowtown would become a real city with people and businesses....and, most importantly, families. He sent Daniel over to get a couple of cups of coffee and while I listened, he talked. Before I knew it, I had been putting that one saddle on that one horse for an entire hour.

I swung into the saddle and headed for the trail, which was about a mile to the east of town. Every time I tried to turn that horse toward the east, his head turned south and before I knew it, I was tied up in front of the

Munger House.

The door swung open with a 'good morning' almost before my first knock.

"You have missed breakfast, Mr. Graham. Mr. Munger, I and the three girls all had things to do early today and when we found your bed empty, we figured you were already on the trail," admonished Mrs. Munger, whom I had never officially met before because of her kitchen duty, "but I can probably find something to put on a plate."

She, too, was tall and stately and it was easy to see where Katie got her stature and her manner. She appeared to be about my age of 36.

"I found your almost empty whiskey bottle in the parlor this morning. Poured the rest of it out and sent the vessel back over to the saloon with Daniel. Would have served no purpose here."

"I'm sorry, Mrs. Munger, I intended to clean up after myself. I just got distracted by other things."

"No particular need to apologize, I'm thinking...except that you brought whiskey into my house and then left it for me to clean up."

"I acknowledge my errors."

"Mr. Munger and I returned home after

the church services later than usual last night as there was a civic discussion about building our city. When we got back, we found Katie awake and serving as guardian for her sleeping sisters."

"I hope my presence in the house didn't create any concerns."

"Not at all. Katie thinks deep. She many times stores up days of thoughts before she visits with us about them. Last night was her time to share. When Katie wants to talk, we listen. She is a strong woman with a strong manner. I'm not sure that is always the best for her, but she is exactly who she is."

"Where is Katie, by the way?"

"She took her sisters over to the school to get ready...said she wanted to talk to the teacher because she is thinking that is something that she might want to do with her life."

"From what little I know of her, I think that is something she would be very good at."

"Yes, probably. She had her 18th birthday a couple of weeks back and immediately set about talking of things she could do and what those things could do to help the town grow. She shares that mission with Darius. She doesn't hold men in very high regard, doesn't trust men much—except for her father, that is."

"During my brief conversation with her, that became pretty obvious."

"I hope she didn't say anything to offend you."

"Not at all, as a matter of fact I found her manner to be refreshing. She is a charming and beautiful young lady."

I finished the bacon, potatoes and coffee which, just as in last night's meal, was well prepared and large in portion, "My compliments on the hospitality and comforts of the Munger House, Mrs. Munger. It has been a pleasure."

"How very nice of you, Mr. Graham...and you need not call me Mrs. Munger, my friends all call me by my first name- Delphi- and I would consider it an honor to call you my friend."

"Thank you, Delphi. I'm afraid I'm burning daylight and must be getting on the way to Lubbock."

"Travel safely, Andy."

"Andy. I like the sound of that. I'm growing more comfortable with being Andy,"

***

The roan was not much easier to get along with when I got on his back. Normally he would fall into a lope naturally, but I couldn't get him to do anything but drag his hooves through the dust, even with investing a great amount of encouragement and noise. It took him five minutes to get to the edge of town and he belligerently stopped at the last water trough. I was leaning on the saddle horn, waiting for him to finish whatever it was he was doing when I became aware of a reflection in the water.

Katie!

That damned horse had brought me to the school.

"Wondered if you would say goodbye," she said quietly.

"Why would you think I wouldn't?"

"You're a man."

"Katie, whatever it was that happened that makes you so sour on men isn't anything that I did, or would do, to you."

"I am beginning to feel that might be true. Had you not sought me out to say goodbye, it would have confirmed my suspicions."

"The horse is smarter than I am," I thought to myself.

"You are a special woman, Katie...a very special woman," I said as I started to dismount.

"You stay in that saddle, Andrew Graham. If you come down here we would end up doing something in public that would probably keep me from becoming a teacher. You just stay put."

"Understood. I agree," I said, as I put myself back in the saddle.

"I hope you plan on coming by this way again."

"I can't promise that I will...but I promise I will think about it, and you, many times."

"If that's the best you can do, I'll accept that."

"It is, for now."

"Goodbye, Andy Graham."

"Goodbye, Katie Munger."

Without a single movement or sound on my part, the roan turned and fell into a lope. We were back on the trail.

ON TO LUBBOCK

It took six more days of hard riding to get to Lubbock. I used that ride to work through the feelings and emotions that came about during my brief visit with the Mungers. Twice I was able to lie to myself about having it all figured out...the last was just before I saw Lubbock once again.

"I should have used that time to figure out how to clear my name," I reprimanded myself.

As I sat there looking at the town, I thought the best thing to do was to ride directly to the Marshal's office and tell them I was an eyewitness to the shooting of the deputy. Hopefully I would get a chance to say what happened and prove I didn't pull the trigger.

My next best idea was to find that lovely young lady and try to make peace with her. If that was to be possible, the next step would be to ask her help in clearing up the situation.

"No, as mad as she was, she just might say I was the shooter just to get her revenge

for my poor judgement."

That's when reality hit me between the eyes, "*What if the deputy died? I guess I just thought he was wounded and recovered. I can still hear the report from the gun. It wasn't large caliber. I don't think so anyway. There was a so much noise in the saloon, how could I tell?*"

As it turns out, I didn't know a damned thing about the outcome or what my situation was even to this very day. Probably the best thing to do was to retreat and return to the mess some other time.

That's right, coward. Run. Hide. Worry. Spend the rest of your life looking over your shoulder to see if a Texas Ranger is following you because they think you shot, or maybe even killed, a deputy.

I had been so involved in learning nothing that I, once again, had failed to hear the hoof beats come up behind me.

"Since Lubbock ain't much to look at, especially from here, can't be the beauty of the city you are takin' in."

The rider was tall and slender...and wearing a silver star on his chest.

"Help you find something...or someone?" he said, all the time his eyes locked on mine.

"Nope. Just restin' and recollectin'."

"So, you been to Lubbock before?"

"Yep. Little over four years now. Stopped in to get something that would wash the trail out of my mouth and, wouldn't you know it, I walked through the swingin' doors when the first punch was thrown in one of the biggest fights I have ever seen. I'll bet there was more than 40 people in that brawl...40 adults and one very pretty little girl and her daddy."

"I know the fight you speak of. Bad deal. Shooting. Lawman died. Talk of a hangin', too."

I felt my heart jump into my throat. *"Lawman DIED?"*

"I had no immediate desire to take part in that fight. So, I turned and walked back to my horse. Heard a gunshot as I got back in the saddle. What happened?"

"Some drover said some unkind things to the young lady, she told her dad and he went looking for the culprit. When Dad did find him, he proceeded to start a fight that he shouldn't have been in. Got schooled, he did."

"Who was it that was shot to death?"

"Nobody. Deputy was wounded in the leg with a shot from a Derringer, but it didn't hardly bleed. There was a former Texas Ranger turned bounty hunter in the saloon and he had been following a fellow from

Tombstone. Guess he thought that with all the confusion it would be a good time to arrest the fellow. When he pulled his pistol, a do-gooder bystander thought he would save the day and pistol-whipped the Ranger. Broke him up pretty good. Died a couple of days later from brain-swelling. At least that's what Doc said caused it."

"Glad I missed all of that. So, whatever became of the little girl and her dad?"

"Well, fact is, she wasn't really a little girl, just looked like it. The guy that came in to defend her virtues wasn't her dad, either. She had run away from her betrothed and arrived a day earlier. She was intent on joining the girls at Polly's. Hank, her boyfriend from Austin, had followed her and had just caught up with her. She told him she had been kidnapped and that the guy responsible was in the bar. They went in the bar, she identified some little fellow at the bar as her kidnapper, Hank went over to waylay him, and all hell broke loose."

"What happened to the guy she identified?"

"With so much fighting going on, who knows what happened to anybody in there. Once that shot rang out everybody left so fast that there was no keeping track of anybody. By the time I checked my wound and I determined I was hardly scratched, let alone going to die, virtually everybody in the building was gone except the people working at Polly's...and somehow, suddenly, they were all deaf, blind, dumb and suffering from amnesia."

"Well, great story, deputy. You tell it very well. I guess, all things considered, the outcome was a good as a person could be hope for."

"Thinkin' you're right. Only person to spend some time in a cell was Hank. He was the one that pulled the trigger on the Derringer. What a waste. Derringers, not Hank. Like swattin' at a hornet. Ain't likely to kill it, just make it mad."

"So is that young lady still at Polly's?"

"Yep. Runs the house."

"Maybe I'll stop down and pay my regards."

"Them girls, they're the curse of the drovers, you know."

"Many times it seems that way."

The deputy sat motionless on his horse, leaning on the saddle horn and looking at me with an inquisitive eye.

"On second thought," I said, "I've got several friends up in Wichita. Think I'll just head up there."

With no direction from me, my horse

wheeled and took to a trot.
   "Damned horse IS smarter than I am."

About the Author

Bob Harvey grew up on a small farm in eastern Colorado.....an arid region that prompted Bob to frequently quip that "you had to work hard just to raise a tumbleweed". The upside of that existence was that he was frequently picking up arrowheads, rusted guns, handcuffs and other historical artifacts that pointed to an earlier time when Native Americans, longhorn steers and drovers roamed the region.

He was a frequent reader of "Red Ryder" novels and comic books and later became a Zane Grey fan. His extensive travels in the states where the Chisholm Trail snaked through the hills and prairies offered opportunities to visit museums and communities where cattle drives were frequent....fostering an increased knowledge of the adventure and danger that was herding cattle.